Blood Rise

Blood Rise

Unflinching Book V

Stuart G. Yates

Also by Stuart G. Yates

'…in the end the law will follow the wrong-doer to a bitter fate, and dishonor and punishment will be the portion of those who sin.'
  — *Allan Pinkerton*

This one is also for Honey, my own White Dove.

Contents

One

On the banks of the Colorado River, where it flows so fast and so wide the far bank might as well be a thousand miles away, a man stooped and cupped his hands, preparing to plunge them into the crystal clear water.

From the rear he appeared a solid-looking man, shoulders bunched with muscle. But from the front, it was clear this man was suffering. His shirt, spattered with crimson, hung from torn trousers, his hair fell lank across his pain-ingrained face and his hands, as they brought the cool water to his broken lips, trembled. Dried blood covered him like a second skin, the largest patch of which spread across his inner thigh. And he was swathed in bandages.

He drank, more water slipping from between his fingers than into his mouth, forcing him to repeat the action, gasping every time. Missing from his right hand were several digits, nothing more than bloody stumps.

A movement from the thick sagebrush caused him to swing around awkwardly. Wincing, for a moment he almost buckled over onto the ground before he used one hand, palm flat against the hard earth, to stop himself . His other squeezed against his thigh.

"You be careful of them stitches, fella," came the voice of an older, gnarled individual, stomping from the brush, a muzzle loading musket draped over his shoulder, two large buck-rabbits in his fist. "I told you to rest."

"I was thirsty," said the man, his voice creaking like a worn, dried-up piece of leather.

"Wait for me next time," said the old man, dropping everything onto the ground. He leaned backwards and stretched out his arms from either side. Bones cracked and he cackled, "Dear God, I am too old for all of this."

"I'll do my share when I can."

"Well, that won't be for best part of a week, fella." He hobbled forward, bow-legged, rocking side to side like a pendulum. "We have a good enough camp here. When you're feeling up to it, we can go down to Twin Buttes and..." He stopped, noting the black cloud settling over the man's face at the mention of the town's name. "Jeez, what the hell is up with you?"

"I'm not going back there," he said, falling down on his backside, staring at the river. He nonchalantly picked up several stones and threw them into the depths one by one.

"Care to tell me why."

"It's a long story."

"Can't be as long as mine."

The man turned to the older one, arching a single eyebrow. "You never did tell me why you saved me."

"Fella, I ain't in the business of detailed explanations. I saw you bleeding to death back at my camp, so I helped you out. Simple as, fella."

"*Your* camp?"

"You heard me. Figured I'd patch you up then, when you is able, you can tell me what in the hell happened back there. And," his hand moved behind his back and when it returned, it was filled with a revolver, "you can explain to me why my daughter was sitting in my shack, dead."

"So you're Dan Stoakes."

"That be me. Who are you?"

"My name's Dixon. I'm a US Marshal out of Fort Bridger. You can check if you like, back at Twin Buttes – but I ain't going there. Not yet."

"A US Marshal..." He rubbed his grizzled chin. "Here's my proposal, fella. I'll make us coffee. Then you tell me your story and I'll tell you mine."

"Sounds like a good enough trade."

"Uh-huh, it is. But you make one move against me, or tell me any lies, and I'll blow your damned head off. You get me?"

"I get you."

Grunting, Dan put the revolver into his waistband and went over to where the fire spat and hissed. With the blaze virtually out, Dan got down on his haunches and revived it, adding more sticks and bracken before dropping lower and blowing at the embers. Once the flames took hold, he set to loading up an old, blackened pot with coffee beans and water and placed it amongst the gathering flames. He sat back. "I need to know how she died."

"She had fever. We'd met and I was accompanying her to your place. To find you, Dan."

"Me?"

"You sent her a telegram, so she told me, of your silver-find. She was on her way when a bunch of cutthroat Indians kidnapped her. But I saved her from them, Dan, helped her with the rest of her journey. Unfortunately, she contracted fever."

He turned his eyes towards Dixon, wide, wet eyes, the anguish clear. "Is that how she died? From fever?"

"I wish to God it was, Dan, but no."

Dan's voice grew close to breaking. He raked in a deep breath. "Tell me."

"I had come across a mighty mean and contentious individual whilst at Bridger. A man I would not wish to turn my back on. He followed us, without my knowledge, and when we reached the camp, he shot me. That was how you found me."

"And my baby girl?"

Dixon lowered his eyes. "He drew down on me, shot away my gun." He held up his shattered hand. "This is the result. He then told me I had to sign over Sarah's claim. When I refused, he smothered her."

"He did *what*?"

"She was so weak she could not resist. He kept his gun on me and put his hand over her mouth and—"

"Stop!" Dan held up his hand, pressing the fingers of his other into his eyes. "Stop, no more. Holy Mother of God … he murdered her."

"That he did. Then he shot me to pieces."

"How – how could a human being be so vile?"

"That is him, I fathom. A vile and detestable sonofabitch. When I see again, I'll kill him."

"No. No you won't. That will be me who does the killing. I'll go into Twin Buttes and shoot that bastard dead."

"He ain't in Twin Buttes any longer, I reckon. He'll be in Glory. He's Sheriff there."

"Is he, by God? Well, I'll set out for Glory and kill him right there. Sheriff – *pah*!" He leaned over, hawked and spat into the dirt. "Murdering bastard. What did you say his name is?"

"I didn't," said Dixon, "but he is well known around these parts as a cruel and callous killer. No one dares cross him."

"Well I dare, damn your hide. *What is his goddamned name?*"

"Simms," said Dixon and hurled the last of his pebbles far out into the churning water of the Colorado River.

Two

They killed them with a knife. The man and the woman, their aged mother and a child, barely 6 months old. Moving out from between the rocks in the early hours, they struck them hard and fast. Curly was the one with the knife, the other two holding down the woman, who kicked and screamed so much Curly was forced to put the blade into her throat.

"Ah, shit, Curly, why do you do that?"

"Shut your face, Brewster," spat Curly, stepping back, watching the woman going into spasm, clutching her throat, dying right there before their eyes.

The sun was barely up over the horizon when they chopped up the woman and put her limbs in a big old pot over the fire.

The third man, a huge hulking brute named Arthur, strangled the old man in the back of the wagon, the baby wailing like a banshee beside him. He smothered the infant with a pillow. It took no more than a few moments. Now he sat stirring the pot, breathing in the aroma. He'd added onions and a carrot that he found in the wagon to the stew. "This is gonna be a feast."

"We ain't eaten nothing but dust for the past six days," said Curly, sitting cross-legged, holding the bloody knife in both hands, "so even if that was horse shit it would taste like it's come from a New York eating house."

"Well it ain't horse shit," said Arthur, "this young lady is nothing but good, lean meat."

"We can make good steaks from her prime, young butt-ocks," said Brewster. "Pity you had to kill her, Curly."

"Shut up, you heathen sap! Killin' is enough for me, it should be for you. I ain't no goddamned fucking rapist."

Brewster remained silent, sinking into himself, staring at the ground.

"And you," said Curly, pointing the blade towards Arthur, "you cook and shut the fuck up."

Arthur touched the brim of his hat and did as Curly bid. He knew better than to argue with Curly 'Lonesome' Price.

"When we broke out," said Brewster when he finally felt able, "you told us there'd be rich pickings for us. You said the same after helping you with that damned stage robbery."

Curly blew out his cheeks. "And there will be rich pickings, Brewster. Now we have this here carbine," he hefted it in his hand, taken from inside the wagon, "life is going to be easier."

"What we gonna do?" asked Arthur, chewing on a piece of flesh.

"There's a town not so very far. It's called Twin Buttes. We can hole up there."

"Is it safe?"

"Safe as anywhere. I know the sheriff there, man name of Silas. We goes back a long ways."

"And how will that help us?"

"He'll give us fresh clothes and horses, and we head deeper into the Territory. There are many towns, most dead, a few dying. Some have banks. We hit 'em hard and we hit 'em fast."

"If they is dead or dying," said Arthur, chewing furiously, "then we ain't likely to find no banks nor no rich pickings, now are we?"

"What are you, Arthur, a goddamned philosopher or somesuch?"

"Stands to reason, Curly. I is just sayin', is all."

"Well don't say nothin'. You have not one clue what awaits us out there in the Territory. Not *one*."

"I hear there is Indians," interjected Brewster, tossing away a gnawed piece of bone. "I hear they is mighty mean too."

"Hell, there is always Indians. Once we are at Twin Buttes, we will stock up with firearms and enough powder to start a war. We will be fine. Besides, I've fought Indians before, and they are not much to be afraid of, I can tell you that. They carry their reputation with 'em like some sort of suit of armour from those old knights in England. They ain't worth shit."

"How you know about those – what was it, *knights*? What the hell is they?"

"You is ignorant, Brewster."

"I is alive."

"Well, that's a topic for discussion right there." Curly hawked and spat. "You have a choice. You can stay out here and fry to death, or you can come with me to Twin Buttes and prosper. I couldn't give a damn either way."

He lay back with his head against a small outcrop of rock and tipped his hat over his eyes. "You just let me know."

Brewster and Arthur exchanged a look. "Ah hell, Curly," said Arthur, "you know we have no choice in the matter."

"Then get some rest. We will cross the prairie at night and keep ourselves out of this heat. I will rise you when it is time to leave."

He wriggled around in the dirt, trying to get comfortable.

Arthur sighed, nodding towards the wagon. "I'm gonna put my head down in there, Brewster."

"Fine, well I will—"

"You will take first watch," said Curly without stirring. "As you say, there is Indians hereabouts."

"Goddamn you both!" spat Brewster, kicking at the ground as Curly rolled over and Arthur wandered across to the wagon. "This ain't fair. Why am I first?"

But there was no reply and he slumped down on a large boulder and munched on the remaining piece of meat from the young girl's arm.

Three

Simms went into town on Monday morning, grimacing with each step his horse took. Having worked all weekend in the raging heat, his back and arms were sore from ploughing through earth as unforgiving as the coarsest, hardest stone.

There were two messages waiting for him. One from his bank, advising him of concerns raised over a land acquisition and a telegram from the Illinois headquarters of the Pinkerton Detective agency. This took most of his attention.

Returning from the Mexican War in Eighteen-Forty-Nine, as news of the California Goldrush hit every headline and passed over every set of lips, Simms found himself taking up work as a detective in the recently formed agency founded by Allan Pinkerton. Now, ten years later, as chief manager of the first eastern branch of the agency, Simms divided his time between his duties as a Pinkerton and that of Sheriff in the town of Glory. Life's curious passage brings with it many unlooked for changes, and so it was with Simms. And often, like now, the weight of responsibility brought profound weariness.

The words of the telegram did not relieve his mood.

'Escaped convicts must be recaught, STOP. Make for Fort Bridger, immediate, STOP. News there. STOP. A.P.'

The route from the town of Bovey to Fort Bridger took two days and, although it followed an old, well-used Indian trail for the most part, danger lurked every step of the way. With this in mind, he unlocked the rifle cabinet and selected his recent acquisition of a Colt Root rifle, with five shots in the cylinder. This allowed him greater firepower than his old Halls carbine, which he affectionately ran his fingers down the stock of before closing up the cabinet once more. At his hip was the Navy Colt given to him by his friend Martinson, who ran an eating-place some distance from the town of Bovey. He had enough paper cartridges for this gun, assembled by his partner White Dove back at the ranch house. He always marvelled at her patience and dexterity at making such fine pieces of ammunition. This cut down on the time it took to reload his sidearm, but even this could not compare to the Smith and Wesson Model One in his shoulder holster. This gun held self-contained metallic cartridges, making reloading fast and effective. So armed he put the coffee pot on the stove and reread the telegram from Illinois one more time.

He sighed. There was still the matter of investigating the Hanrahan funeral robbery. Ruminating on what to do for the best, he barely had enough time to throw down a cup of half-brewed coffee before he climbed into his saddle and cantered across to the big old house on the outskirts of town to talk to the deceased's surviving offspring.

The daughter of the deceased greeted him at the door. Doffing his hat, Simms stepped inside, his dust-caked boots sounding hollow on the entrance hall's floorboards. He smiled to her, somewhat self-consciously, as a young maid emerged and stooped down next to him with dustpan and brush. "My apologies."

"Don't trouble yourself none, Detective," said the daughter, and beckoned him to move farther inside. "Betsy, make us some coffee after you've cleaned up."

The maid nodded and Simms gave her an apologetic smile which she did not return.

He followed the daughter into the parlour, a large room with chintz-covered couch, writing table and straight-backed chair in the corner. The fireplace, although empty, bore the marks of recent use. Twin patio doors opened up to an impressive back yard, with mature trees and flower beds. An air of tempered opulence hung over the room., as it did much of the rest of the impressively decorated house.

Taking his attention were the wallpaper designs, rendered in powder-blue with a floral motif. He leaned across and peered at a section closely.

"You are interested in such decoration, Detective?"

"I am indeed, Miss ...?" He looked at her from over his shoulder.

"My name is Naomi." She held out her hand. Simms straightened and took it, wondering if he should kiss it in the old-fashioned way. He'd heard it was appropriate in certain sectors of society. He decided against it. "I am the second of my late father's four daughters. Elspeth, the eldest, is seeing to some of the legal wrangling associated with my father's estate, whilst my—"

"Forgive me, Miss Naomi, but my time is pressing. I need to know what happened."

"Oh, I see." She grew a little flustered, a slight reddening appearing around her jaw. "Well, I suppose we will start here as this is where my father lay." Waving her arms vaguely towards the patio doors, she pressed the back of the same hand to her mouth, eyes closed, and swallowed down a tiny sob. "I'm sorry."

"Perhaps I should come back at another time, when you are feeling more at ease."

He held his breath. He wanted this case done and dusted before he set-out for Bridger. Escaped convicts were more pressing than a simple robbery. Or so he assumed.

"No, no," she said quickly, producing a silken handkerchief from inside her sleeve. Dabbing her eyes, she forced a tight smile. "It's all been – well, *hectic* is the word I suppose you could use, Daddy struck down so quickly, you see. Unexpected."

Simms caught his breath, his interest tweaked. "Oh? I didn't know that. I assumed he was ill."

"Daddy was at his fittest for years," Naomi said, pausing a moment to dab her eyes again. "He had begun socialising with a group of like-minded landowners and would often invite them here for dinner. At one such meeting, he grew to be very fond of a widow from town. A Mrs Miller, who had lost her husband some years back from—"

"Excuse me, did you say Mrs *Miller*. Mrs Laura Miller, from the town of Glory?"

"Yes, that's her. Do you know her, Detective? An extremely handsome and affectionate woman, whom Daddy took a shine to almost as soon as she appeared on our front porch." She giggled at the memory, her eyes growing distant, "She imbued him with a new lease of life, Detective. I have not seen him as happy for many years, not since Mama died."

Reflecting on these revelations, Simms wandered across to the porch doors and looked out towards the manicured lawn. "And the robbery, Miss Naomi? What happened exactly?"

"Well, people were coming and going. Jacob, our manservant, did the best he could, but we had no way of knowing who came to pay their last respects."

He turned, staring at her. A fragile little thing, pasty-faced, awash with grief. "Could you possibly make a list of everything that was taken?"

"Yes, I can do that. Somebody must have slipped upstairs to Mama's room. All of her jewellery…" She coughed, again the handkerchief pressing against her face. "Poor Daddy. I thank God he didn't have to suffer any of that."

"I think, perhaps, if he hadn't suffered the way he did, none of this would have happened."

"I don't understand you, Detective."

"As ghastly as it may sound, there are professional thieves out there who prey on people when they are at their lowest – funerals being the main one. They also frequent society weddings, sometimes purporting to be newspeople looking to report the event. However they do it, they get inside and help themselves to whatever they can find. This theft is clearly in the same mode."

"I see. But yes, you are quite right, Detective – it is ghastly."

"If you could make up the list, send it over to my office, I would be obliged. And if you can cast your mind back, try to think of any *strangers* you may have noticed. A couple perhaps."

"A couple?"

"Yes, they often work in pairs. A man and woman, full of grief, draped in black, the woman probably wailing, the man standing apart, serious."

"Dear Lord, as if such a thing could happen."

"All too often, Miss Naomi, it does." He touched the brim of his hat. "Please get those scraps of information to me, no matter how insignificant they may seem."

"I will, Detective." She reached out and touched his arm as he went to move to the door. "Thank you. All of this, at such a time..."

He smiled knowingly, nodded and walked out.

Stepping out onto the porch, the heat hit him like a door slamming in his face. He hauled himself into his saddle and gently turned the horse away. The maid gave him a small wave and he tipped his hat in response and spurred his mount into a canter.

All the while, on his ride back to Bovey, a single thought burrowed its way deeper into his brain.

Laura Miller knew Randolph Hanrahan.

And now Randolph Hanrahan was dead.

Four

After Dixon told the old man his abbreviated and heavily altered story, he slumped back against a boulder, blowing out a long, meaningful sigh. "If I could have saved her, Dan, I would have."

The old man sat some way opposite, the big old musket across his lap, chewing at a piece of dried-up grass, running through the Marshal's words, not giving anything away by his expression, allowing the seconds to tick idly by. Dixon shifted and was about to speak again when the old man held up his hand, cutting him off. "My daughter was a courageous girl. Strong, intelligent. She'd made something of herself over in Kansas City before that feather-brained bastard of a husband left her when she fell pregnant. Bradford Milligan his name was. A waster, a shirker, a spineless bastard. As soon as he done the deed, off he shot like a prairie turkey running from a fox." He leaned to his right and spat. "If I find him, I'll kill him."

"But your daughter made good – you said so yourself."

"Yes she did. And I am mighty proud of her." His eyes glazed over for a moment, a sudden thought striking him. He swallowed hard. "*Was* mighty proud of her. Now she has gone. And this varmint, this – what did you say his name was again?"

"Simms. Sheriff over in Glory."

"I ain't ever been to Glory, but I have a mind to now. Why would he kill her?"

Dixon shrugged. "To claim the silver, I shouldn't wonder."

13

"Well, I'll check on that. Mister, you appear genuine, but I have lived a long time and been through some scrapes ..." He patted his side to give emphasis to his words. "Those two bushwhackers thought they'd killed me when they came into my camp and took over. Shot me. Fortunately, I fell into the river and it carried me off downstream. I didn't trust them and I don't trust you."

"Well, I don't see why not, because I—"

"Because of this." He pulled out a soiled and torn piece of paper. He waved it in his hand. "This here is a claim on *my* silver mine, which I found in your jacket. It says you is the rightful owner of said claim, counter-signed by the assayer office down in Twin Buttes. At the bottom," he tapped the paper, "are three more signatures – those of the claimants. I can just make out your name here. Dixon. And beside it, that of my daughter and that of the witness." He swung the musket around. "You is one lying sonofabitch and now you're gonna die."

Cracking his hip on large, jagged pieces of rock, Dixon rolled across the broken ground as quickly as he could. He felt several of his wounds opening up, but he had no time for such trivialities. Not now, as the musket boomed, sending a piece of hot lead screeching inches from his head.

Old Dan worked frantically at the ramrod, knowing time was against him.

Time he simply did not have. He looked up frantic and went for the revolver in his belt.

As Dixon put his boot under the old man's chin and rocketed him onto his back, Dan knew the end had come.

This time there would be no river to enable escape. To save his life.

Dixon wrenched the musket from Dan's feeble grip and put the stock into the old man's face half a dozen times, smashing it to pieces, not stopping until the brains mingled with the many pieces of bone fragments, facial features broken and unrecognisable.

Stepping away, breathing hard, Dixon flung the musket away, bent double and vomited into the dirt.

Then came the pain and he checked his wounds and groaned. Blood oozed between the stitches Dan had so expertly applied. The patched-up areas where Simms's bullets had penetrated, the final one in his inner thigh, designed to let him bleed out. Checking this one, Dixon sighed in relief. It remained closed.

Stumbling across to Dan Stoakes's meagre belongings, he scooped up the canteen and drained it, drinking without pause, gasping when at last he stopped.

Above him the buzzards circled already, preparing to settle on old Dan. Dixon went to the body and, turning away from the ruined head, found the paper and knocked away the bits of brain matter clinging to the edge. He folded it carefully and put it inside his vest. He took the revolver and checked it. One chamber loaded, but with no percussion cap. As good as useless, he flung it away in despair.

After filling up the canteen from the river, he realised there was nothing else to do now but try and find a way back to Twin Buttes. He didn't wish to go, but the choices he may once have had now lay dead along with the old man. Dan's mule stood some distance away, forlorn, shrunken, the bones of its ribs sticking out from the thin flesh. Dixon sighed. It was the best he had.

He took the musket and loaded it with shot from the tiny bag at Dan's hip. Four more pieces of lead and a small quantity of powder remained. He took the bag and went to the mule, stroking its neck before hauling himself up over its back. Never having ridden a mule before, he had little idea what it might be like. No saddle, a threadbare rope bridle and rein, with no stirrups. Slow and easy would be the order of the day.

If he ever got the damned thing moving.

He kicked, cajoled, swore and cooed. Nothing worked. The mule remained sullen, silent and still. Cursing, after a final kick, Dixon slid from the animals back. "You rangy bastard," he drawled. The mule merely looked.

Settling the musket across his back by the strap, he set off towards the tree line. With little idea what direction he was taking he didn't give much for his chances, but he tramped on nevertheless, doing his best to ignore the leaking wounds and the throbbing bruises. He may well be dead before nightfall.

And to give credence to his thoughts, a quick glance back to the makeshift camp told him how fragile the line between life and death was, as the buzzards settled upon old Dan and feasted on his flesh. He shuddered, hunched up his shoulders and pushed into the depths of the forest, leaving the charnel house scene far behind.

Five

The homestead stood deserted, wall planks buckled, some fallen into the ground. An old rocking chair , painted white, sat on the porch , the only evidence that people ever dwelt here.

There were four buildings. A main house, two barns and an out-house, or privy. Wind moaned through the broken doors of the main barn, sending up flurries of hay and straw. Horses stabled here once, their ghosts lingering in the thick, musty smell, sunlight from a roof light cutting thin beams through the floating dust.

Nothing lived here now except the silence.

Curly, bent low behind a small rise, scanned every inch of the place, not convinced it was uninhabited.

"It's clearly deserted," said Arthur. Next to him, Brewster stretched himself out on the ground, arms behind his head, hat over his eyes. "What do you think, Brewster?"

"I think we wait until nightfall. Safer that way."

"He's right," said Arthur enthusiastically. "Damn it, Curly, it can only be a couple of hours or so before evening. Let's wait it out."

Curly spat into the dirt, checking the carbine's load for the umpteenth time. "It's as dead as poor Brewster's winky. I say we go take a look."

"My winky ain't dead!"

Both of the others exchanged a quick look and burst into laughter. "It's a good as, Brewster," spluttered Arthur. "Don't think I have ever seen anything so small!"

"Fuck you, Arthur," said Brewster, sitting up. "I ain't ever had no complaints."

"Is that true?" Curly put in, twisting up the side of his mouth in doubt. "You ever been with a woman, Brewster?"

"Course I have."

"When?"

"Eh? *When*? Well, I...I don't rightly recall, but I have – lots of times."

"In prison?"

Brewster shot Arthur a sharp look. "What in the hell do you mean by that?"

"What I say – you had any women in prison?"

"Well how in the hell am I supposed to have done that? There ain't *no women in prison*."

Arthur nodded, shrugged and turned to Curly. "He's been in and out of prison since he was seven years old. Spent more time *inside* than he has out."

"More *in* prison, than in a woman, eh Brewster?"

They roared and Brewster pulled down his hat and turned his back on them. "Pair of miserable bastards. What if I am a virgin, it don't mean I have a tiny winky."

"No, it don't," said Arthur. "But you do."

Another burst of laughter and then Arthur spotted a figure running in a half-crouch from the smaller of the two barns towards the back of the house. "Holy shit," he said, dropping down out of sight. "There is someone there, Curly."

Cursing, Curly slid out the knife from its sheath and handed it over to Arthur. "Could be an Indian."

"Whoever or whatever, we'd best be careful."

Curly grinned. "You're damn right. And so are you Brewster – we wait until dark."

Night seemed a long time coming. With nothing to do except snooze, every passing minute seemed like an hour, and when Curly finally did poke his head over the rim of the small dip they were lying in and saw the horizon streaked with purple and orange he let out a whoop of relief.

"Another hour," came Brewster's voice from beneath his hat.

"We can move now," said Curly stretching out his legs.

"Best take no chances. It needs to be totally black, Curly."

"You ain't nothing but an old woman, Brewster, and a damned finicky one at that."

"Whoever is down there is probably covering the approach to the house right this moment. If we go there now, one of us is likely to get shot."

Slumping back down, Curly, acting like an admonished child, folded his arms and sulked. "If I had another gun we could—"

"But you ain't," said Arthur. "Best do as Brewster says. We wait."

So they did. In silence. And when deep, inky black replaced the smudges of burnished purple across the sky, Curly rolled over the lip and scurried down to the house, carbine in hand, Arthur a little behind.

They made it to the door without incident, both of them crouching low, straining to listen.

Padding softly across the open ground came Brewster and, when he reached the others, they all waited, breathing low. The sky, crystal clear, stretched above them, alive with stars, allowing for ample illumination of their surroundings.

Curly, gripping the carbine, made to put his hand on the door handle, but Arthur was there first, the index finger of his other hand pressed to his lips. Gesticulating towards the barns, he gestured for Curly to scoot around the back. Curly nodded, exchanged the gun for the knife Arthur held and loped off into the darkness.

Looking at Brewster, Arthur winked and tried the handle.

It turned down, making a slight creak, and the door inched open.

Grunting with satisfaction, Arthur pulled open the door fully and went to step inside.

The shotgun blast took him full in the midriff, hurling him backwards to the ground where he lay, sprawled out, bewildered, his vest spattered with a myriad of tiny red dots.

"Scatter gun," wheezed Brewster and stood up, preparing to retreat.

He froze when a figure emerged through the door, the shotgun already broken, spent cartridges flying away, new ones slipped into the chambers. The solid clunk of the barrels engaging and Brewster was screaming as he turned. The blast hit him between the shoulders and he fell face-first into the dirt as if kicked by a mule.

Curly, moving like a cat, padded across the room and, as the figure ejected two more cartridges, he got his left arm around the person's throat and put the knife into its back. Four times, each stab quick and decisive, dropping it to the floor where it writhed for a moment before growing still.

Without pausing, Curly took up the shotgun and the two new cartridges lying next to the body and loaded up the gun once more. Then he stood, dragging in his breath, peering out into the clear night to see both his companions lying on the ground, groaning in agony and disbelief.

His own disbelief, coupled with developing shock, buckled his knees, the strength draining from his body as he fell onto his backside and broke down in body-jerking sobs.

Six

"I may as well come right out and say it," said Major Porter of the U.S. Army from behind his desk at Fort Bridger, a ramrod-stiff lieutenant standing next to him, staring into the distance, "I don't like you."

"Feeling's mutual," said Simms, voice flat. "Just give me the Colonel's notifications, then I'll be on my way."

"I am still not convinced of your innocence over the murder of one of my men, Simms. But you have convinced everyone else of your innocence, so I am powerless to see justice done. You seem to have some hold over Colonel Johnstone, although what it is I fail to comprehend, and have bent him to your will."

Letting out a long breath, Simms stared hard into the Major's eyes. "The notifications, Porter, or I'll find them myself."

Porter, loath to back down too quickly, leaned back in his chair and folded his arms. Without turning his eyes away, he said, "Give him the papers, Lieutenant."

Simms took them from the Lieutenant's outstretched hand and immediately read them. When he finished, he looked again at Porter. "You know what this says, of course."

"Of course. But I can't spare you any men."

"That's not what it says here."

"No, but the situation has changed. The Colonel has taken a troop into the interior once again. Not Mormons this time, but Bannocks.

Seems they are on the move and have already overrun two home-steads. It appears their so-called truce with the Latter Days is over."

"Something must have stirred them up."

"Starvation," said the Lieutenant. The others looked at him keenly. He stiffened a little more, a reddening appearing around his jowls. "A group of Kiowa came in a few nights ago, no more than twenty of them. I've never seen such a rangy bunch. They told me the rains had not fallen all winter and game was scarce. So scarce many of their children had already died, so they came here in desperation."

"You speak Kiowa? That's quite an accomplishment."

"My father was a Colonel in the Army some twenty or so years ago, sir. Took part in the early wars with those people. He taught me what he could."

Nodding, Simms folded up the papers and put them inside his coat. "I'm impressed, Lieutenant, but I doubt if Bannocks will come here seeking the same. Nor the Utes or Shoshone. They'll all be starving, desperate to take whatever they can."

"I've also heard people are turning to cannibalism right across the Territory."

Simms shivered, recalling the scenes he witnessed not so long ago – an entire family butchered and eaten, how, after meeting up with the perpetrators, circumstances led him to confrontation and, of course, killing. Always the killing.

"Those three men," said Porter sharply, "one of them had something to do with the incident involving Senator Bowen. Washington don't give two hoots about the others, but they want him taken back alive."

"Which one?"

Porter shrugged. "No idea. They didn't say."

"Or if they did, you have conveniently forgotten his name."

"Now why in the hell would I do that?"

"Oh, I don't know, just some sick notion of yours to put me in the shit if I happen to kill them all."

Porter smirked. "Good luck, Detective, in hunting down those es-capees – I think you're gonna need it."

Simms met up with Deep Water a day's ride from Bridger, the detective taking time to read what the message said to his friend.

"They broke out four days ago," said Simms, "and it seems they headed west, cutting across the prairie on foot."

"They could not have gone far," said the scout.

They sat astride their respective mounts, soaring peaks forming a backdrop to the vast wilderness stretching out before them. Occasional patches of scrub and outcrops of rock punctuated the vista, affording some relief from the burning sun. Arriving early, the summer-scorched earth already barren from lack of rain, seemed to moan in pain due to the unrelenting heat. Everything baked, including Simms who sat in shirt sleeves, mopping his brow with his neckerchief. "If they are exposed to this sun for any amount of time, they will already have dropped down dead from exhaustion."

"There are few directions they could have come. Unless they have found themselves horses, I will have little problem picking up their trail."

"That's what I was hoping you'd say."

Exchanging knowing smiles, they swung around and made steady progress in the direction of the state prison, newly built some twenty or so miles north of Bridger.

Simms spotted the ragged line of warriors through his German-made field-glasses. Both men had dismounted, scurrying across the scrub to find a decent vantage point.

"Hunting party," breathed Simms and passed the glass to his friend. Deep Water frowned, studying the precision-made instrument with some respect before putting it to his eyes.

"War party," he said. "I count ten. Three, maybe four have rifles. Four share two horses. I cannot tell if they are Bannock or Ute."

"The Major told of Bannocks raiding homesteads. This could be the same bunch."

"Maybe." Deep Water studied the glasses again. "These are magical things, my friend. How is it possible to see so far?"

"I have no idea," said Simms, taking them back and dropping them into their case. "Got them from a Mexican officer way back. They've served me well since." Another look towards the group of warriors. "You think we should shadow them?"

Deep Water grunted. "From the signs I see, those escaped men, they head across open prairie. If the war-party spot them, as they surely will, you have lost your chance of taking the men alive."

"You think they have picked up their trail also?"

"It could be. Not many cut across open prairie in this heat."

"So, they could be our salvation and lead us straight to our quarry."

"If those warriors do not get to the men you seek first."

Rubbing his face, Simms rolled over onto his back. "That would suit Porter just fine. He's still smarting after I was proved innocent of killing a trooper back in Bridger earlier this year. They tried to frame me. Not sure if Proctor was in on it, but he sure as hell was eager to get my neck in a noose."

"So who did try and frame you?"

"Guy name of Dixon. He was a US Marshal."

"A US Marshal tried to frame you for murder? Why?"

"He had some deal going on, thought I might sniff it all out. Least-ways, it all went right in the end."

"You killed him?"

Simms smiled. "As good as."

"What does that mean?"

"It means I left him to bleed to death. After what he'd done, I thought it best for him to suffer."

"But how do you know he is dead?"

Simms arched an eyebrow. "Can't see anyone surviving a bullet in the thigh, can you?"

Looking away, Deep Water remained silent and reflective.

Propping himself up on his elbows, Simms peered towards his old friend. "You have known of such a thing?"

"Yes. I have known of such a thing."

These words caused Simms a touch of concern and he tried to busy himself by dusting away at his pants and checking his firearms. He took his time, trying his best not to reveal the concern developing inside. But no matter what he did, Deep Water's words percolated away and he wondered if Dixon may well have survived. If he had, then the open expanse of the Territory held more dangers than he had first envisaged.

Seven

He emerged from the trees as the first cold light of dawn seeped out from between a sky stricken with grey clouds. He stopped and frowned. For weeks, possibly months, no rain fell to give respite to earth hard and compacted. Plants withered, birds stopped singing and, despite the Colorado flowing so freely and so full, he often wondered if there might be a time when even that mighty river would dry up.

But not today.

He heard the deep and distant rumble of thunder.

A storm was coming and he gritted his teeth and considered returning to the trees to take shelter. Something stirred, an old tale of lightning striking trees and killing folk. He thought he might take his chances. And then he saw the deer.

It stood, grazing on the few sparse pieces of scrub, rummaging for a new shoot, something soft, green. With ears constantly flicking, a tremor running across its flanks, all senses were on high alert. But hunger made it careless and Dixon was downwind. Caressing the stock of his musket, he slowly checked the load, brought the gun up to his shoulder and sighted down the barrel. He had one shot. If he missed, the animal would break and run, giving him no chance of a second shot even if he could load it in time, which he doubted.

He sucked in a breath and held it.

And then he heard the faintest snap of a branch from somewhere to his right.

He froze.

So did the deer, its head snapping up as if on a taut, steel spring. All thought of food now forgotten, it moved, a blur of engaged muscle, veering away from the sound, bounding out of range even as the arrow soared through the air and landed harmlessly where the deer had stood not seconds before.

Dixon went into a low crouch, making himself as small as possible between a gathering of broken boulders, holding his breath.

They came into view. Three young bucks, torsos bare, wearing breechclouts and fringed leggings, moved stealthily forward. Two were armed with bows, already nocked, the third holding a long lance, perhaps to despatch the deer once felled by an arrow.

Dixon flattened himself on the ground, mouth open, controlling his breathing. The musket could kill one, but then what would he do? They'd be on him in a blink, slitting his throat and feasting on his innards before he knew what hit him. So he waited. Sweat rolled down his forehead and dripped into his eye, but he dare not raise a hand to wipe it away .

The three warriors crept forward, searching the wide plain ahead. One came within six paces from where Dixon lay. He closed his eyes, held his breath. Dear God, if they saw him...

A sharp shout and Dixon almost cried out, expecting it to be a cry of alarm, raised by the one who spotted him. He chanced a look, hoping against hope it would not be his last. He saw them straighten their backs, the disappointment clear in their voices as they barked more words to one another.

One pointed towards the far horizon and his companions muttered guttural grunts. Dixon cursed himself for not taking more notice of their language. A single, recognisable word might give him some clue what caused them such anxiety.

For they were anxious.

And when he opened both eyes and peered across the plain, he understood why.

Horses. A line of approaching men, mere black smudges as yet but moving ever closer.

The three warriors, agitated and alarmed, turned on their heels, readying to dive back amongst the trees and out of sight.

And then one of them spotted him.

In that single glance something substantial passed between them.

A look of sheer, penetrating hatred.

Dixon fumbled for the musket but squeezing the trigger with his third finger always proved difficult. So little strength in it. He tried his best. And his best simply was not good enough.

His incapacity saved him.

In those long drawn out seconds, with the horses pounding ever closer, the warrior swung away, making his fateful decision, plunging into the undergrowth behind his fellow braves.

Dixon allowed his breath to dwindle out in a long stream and he rolled onto his back and prayed to God that the others, the pounding of their mounts almost upon him, would not see him.

Ponies snorted close by, the tang of human sweat wafting over him, the sound of feet dropping to the ground.

They were close, fanning out in a thin line, moving cautiously forward. One or two whispered comments, words as unfamiliar as the ones he had listened to earlier. He closed his eyes, clutching the musket close to his chest, not believing danger to be so close for a second time in only a few moments.

A foot fell so close. He fought back the urge to look, hoping against hope the dry grass and scrub in which he lay would cover him sufficiently. It had not done so before, when the other brave spotted him.

He knew it was only a matter of time. And if there might have been a slight chance of overcoming the first group, he knew now he could do nothing against these – there were too many.

With heartbeat pounding so hard he felt sure they would hear, he tried his utmost to keep his breathing steady.

A movement. To his left. Quickening heart, sweat running down to drip onto the ground beside him. A whiff of a breeze, a memory of past times, youth, the mind regressing before the darkness closed in. The precursor to death.

They moved on towards the trees, ignoring him, not noticing him. The tramp of their footfalls growing fainter.

He waited, counting the seconds. If he moved too soon they would hear him, return and hack off the top of his head.

Thirty seconds, then a minute. Two. Eyes closed, ticking off the seconds.

At three minutes, he sat up.

They were nowhere. He squinted into the depths of the wood. They were in pursuit of the others. Indians who hated other Indians. A curious fact, one which he never fully grasped.

Clambering to his feet, he straightened out his back and turned away from the wood.

An Indian stood, caring for the horses, with his back to Dixon, looking out across the prairie, perhaps searching for something or someone.

Frozen, Dixon slowly brought the musket up, sighting along the barrel. One shot, then a mad dash away, away across the prairie to safety.

As he took a first, tentative step to decrease the range between himself and the waiting Indian, his boot came down on the dried, brittle bracken, causing it to snap as loud as any gunshot.

The Indian turned. Time stopped. Silence fell. And Dixon charged.

Reacting, the warrior brought out his knife and hatchet, tensing himself but, taken by surprise, he could do nothing to prevent Dixon from swinging the musket across the side of his head, smashing him to the ground where he lay, stunned and bleeding. The ponies immediately went into hysterics, kicking and screaming, and Dixon, not waiting to see what horrors might be bearing down on him from the trees, jumped up onto the back of the nearest animal and kicked it hard in the flank. The mule, which he'd left far behind, would never have given him such hope for a successful escape, but the pony proved different. Small and powerful, it broke into a mad, stampeding gallop and Dixon clung on, musket across his back, hands gripping the animal's mane, flattening himself low against its neck.

It thundered over the plain but already he heard the whoops and cries from behind him. Straining his back and neck, he chanced a look behind and saw the warriors running around the other hysterical ponies, trying to calm them, several warriors managing to haul themselves up onto their backs. Soon the pursuit would be on and Dixon held fast, his cheek pressed close to the pony, his eyes closed, hoping to God he could make higher ground, gain an advantage, do his utmost to hold them off before they got too close. An arrow in the back was not how he wanted his life to end, not after coming so far, surviving so much.

Dixon kept his eyes fixed on the rapidly moving ground beneath him as the pony's hooves stomped across the hard ground in a blur. All he needed to do was keep going for as long as he could.

Craning his neck, he spotted the buttes ahead, yellow and white rocks sprouting from the barren earth, soaring high enough for him to hold out, send a few well-aimed pieces of lead in the direction of his pursuers. Dissuade them. Force them to reconsider, if only for a moment.

All he needed to do was keep going.

But as he tugged at the pony's mane, attempting to turn the animal, it fought against him and went into a wild bronco-dance, screaming its protest, kicking out with its hind legs. Not the response he expected nor needed. With no saddle, stirrups, and the flimsiest of rope bridles, he knew he had little hope of remaining astride the beast.

If he fell, he might break his neck or his back.

Either would be preferable to what awaited him from his Indian pursuers.

He clung on, desperate, every fibre of his body straining, every muscle burning, but his old wounds would not allow him to remain on the animal's back. His first two fingers were missing from his right hand, but his other fared little better. Both hands, slick with sweat, slid from the bridle rope, making it impossible to stay astride the animal. As the pony checked its forward motion and reared up, lashing out its forelegs in angry protest, Dixon sent out a desperate prayer, his body slipping to the left. Soon he would crash to the dirt and any hope of making the buttes would be lost.

Gritting his teeth, the pony jumping, bucking, sending out clouds of dust beneath it, Dixon's mind reeled with visions of savage faces and evil, glinting blades. Left hand held on to the mane, right hand no longer able to hold on. Inner thigh and shoulder screamed, old Dan's handy work with sewing needle and thread coming apart, pain returning, the blood leaking.

He had no other option than to fall.

And so he did.

Eight

The morning found him sitting in the same position, staring into the distance, eyes full of grit due to lack of sleep, but he didn't care.

Looking across to the body, surrounded by a pool of black blood, he felt numb. As the daylight streamed through the door, he made out her details for the first time. A young woman, long flaxen hair trailing down her back, one arm reaching out, the hand frozen in a gesture of pleading. Pleading for her life. The life Curly took away.

He stood up, legs still unsteady, stepped out into the open and took a breath. His two companions remained as they fell, both moaning. He gave Arthur a cursory glance and went over to Brewster. The buckshot spread across his back, high up, between the shoulder blades. Clicking his tongue, Curly scanned the surroundings, his natural instincts telling him the woman could not be alone. But any friends, if there were any, surely could not be close. If this were so, they would have attacked already. So, easing out a breath, he got down on his knees, whispering, "You'll be just fine, old friend. Just hold on."

For Arthur, however, things were very different. Already ashen, face taking on a waxy sheen, when Curly moved closer it was clear Arthur was close to death. His stomach was so shot up it bore the resemblance to a kitchen sieve, the bloody flesh perforated with buckshot. He took the blast full on, unlike Brewster, whose frantic efforts at retreat had saved him.

Curly put his palm on Arthur's brow. "I'm sorry," he said. "I will do the best I can."

He laboured for the next hour or more, taking each body into the building, ignoring their squeals as he dragged them across the dirt, bumping them up the steps and into the parlour. He lay them both down on the floor and built up the fire. In the kitchen he found pieces of cutlery and set to work on Brewster's back. Pulling the torn and ragged vest apart, his friend let loose a string of howls and curses but Curly set to work nevertheless, picking out the buckshot piece by piece with an old fork.

When finished, Curly laid strips of damp rags across the many tiny holes, soaking up the seeping blood, hoping infection would not kick in. He knew a little about infection, having seen men in the past dying from the most innocuous of wounds as they festered, turning yellow, flesh swelling purple and black. Not understanding any of it, all he knew was the cleaner the wound the better.

But for poor old Arthur, no amount of cleaning was going to save him.

His eyes were wild, red-rimmed, lips blue, flesh white as chalk. And the sweat. Dear God Almighty, his face and body were alive with it.

"I'll keep you as comfortable as I can," said Curly, kneeling next to his friend, "but Arthur, I cannot save you."

Arthur writhed, gnashing his teeth. "You bastard, Curly. I'll live you out, see if I don't."

Shaking his head, Curly let out a long sigh. "I doubt it." He turned away and looked towards the open fire, and the blackened pot set upon the stack of burning wood, bubbling away, the contents rousing his taste buds, the saliva trickling from his mouth in anticipation of the flavours and tastes to come. "I wonder why she was here, all on her lonesome." He went across to the open door and looked out. "We've got four shells," he said, patting the shotgun he held in the crook of his arm, "and one in the carbine. I don't think that's enough. Her companions are out there, I can feel it."

Behind him Brewster stirred, moaning. "Perhaps they have moved on – or have died."

Curly shook his head, without turning, his voice small and strained. "Or maybe they are planning on coming back. What we don't know is when..."

Later than afternoon, Arthur grew delirious, screaming incoherently, body thrashing, the blood bubbling. Teeth gnashing, alive with pain, his eyes boiled in his head. Curly took the decision and put the only round in the carbine through his friend's brain and stood and stared for a long time.

Curly buried Arthur around the back of the house, fashioning a primitive cross from old pieces of wood he found. He stood and surveyed his work, the mound of earth marking Arthur's place. Prayers were not something that Curly knew much about, but he knew he should say something. He looked up and smiled. "Arthur, you and me, we were never that close. Back when we tried to take that stage, you cursed me for everything that went wrong. I don't blame you. Maybe, if I had not taken up the offer, we wouldn't be where we are right now and you would still be alive. Who can say? Life is not something you can depend on, that is for sure. Our time here is limited, and we do what we can, and not all of it turns out as we planned. I'm sorry I got you killed, old friend. Wherever you are, you take care."

Pleased with himself, he took up the shotgun and spade and tramped back into the house, keeping his eye on the tree line, knowing full well that when they did come, they would be hell bent on killing. And joining Arthur in his journey to the Hereafter was not something he planned on doing... at least not yet.

Nine

Dixon ran, head down, arms pumping, forcing his legs to move through sheer willpower, ignoring the pain until even his determination to survive gave way and he fell, exhausted, to the ground.

Sucking in his breath, he rolled over onto his belly. Two bucks were closing fast, whooping, sensing victory. Flattening himself, Dixon eased the musket around and took careful aim, settling his breathing, the pounding of his heart, fear rippling through every fibre.

He waited, knowing his single shot had to count. There would be no time to reload. They came on, beating the rumps of their mounts, gathering speed.

So close now, the taste of their sweat hitting the back of his throat. Young warriors, burnished bodies shiny with sweat, muscles rippling, desperate to make their kill.

The lead buck was breathtaking in his beauty, smooth faced, eyes so wide, all his life ahead of him. A mouth made to pleasure his woman, so full, peerless. No more than eighteen.

Dixon shot him in the chest, the blast hurling the young warrior from the back of his horse, dumping him unceremoniously into the dirt.

Moving fast, Dixon reared up, taking the musket by the barrel and, using it as a club, he swung hard, landing a massive blow across the second young man's midsection, swiping him off his pony.

With no time to admire his handiwork, Dixon stumbled on towards the towering rocks, the pain too great now to allow him to run. He reached the first boulders and scrambled over them, slipping, cracking his knees against the coarse hardness of the surface. Cursing, he nevertheless pressed on, aware he could not afford to stop, and reached the base of the large outcrop soaring above him. Looking up, he searched for footholds and handholds, looped his arm through the musket strap and started the climb.

His plan was a simple one – reach a ledge, high enough to allow him an advantage, reload and shoot as many as his powder allowed. Better that than to sit out on the prairie and die in the most horrific of ways. They would strip him, split his balls and peg him out to die in the searing heat. Such stories filtered into places like Fort Bridger, told by pilgrims and trappers lucky enough to have survived. People said Comanches were the worst, that they were moving up from Texas, desperate for food as the drought tightened its grip. Worse than that of Fifty-Seven, so those who knew about such things said. Dixon knew nothing of that. Back then, he was in Kansas, doing his job. US Marshal. What he wouldn't give to be there now.

He hawked and spat, hauling himself up one more inch. He was taking too long and, for all he knew, the young buck he knocked down was already on his feet, recovered. He should've taken the time to cave the bastard's head in.

He really should've taken the time.

Below him, he heard it. The grunting as his pursuer moved ever closer.

Dixon looked down and cursed.

Younger, swifter, stronger, the buck was gaining on him, negotiating the rock face with all the skill of a mountain goat. Fearless, dismissive of danger, he proved a terrifying sight. In a man-to-man fight, Dixon knew he wouldn't stand a chance against him, his only real hope to continue climbing, to put as much distance as he could between them, to find that elusive ledge, charge his musket and blow the Indian's head off.

If he could make that ledge. If he could find it.

There was only a matter of a few yards between them now, the buck so nimble and Dixon feeling his age, swallowing down the pain from his many wounds. He should never have left Dan at the river to die, perhaps made a deal with the old coot, help him to have his revenge on Simms. Anything but this. Groaning with the effort, he forced himself to continue.

His fingers curled around a jagged piece of rock and he hauled himself up, managing to get a foothold inside a tiny crack. And there it was – a ledge. He almost whooped with joy but it caught in his throat as another quick look behind him proved there would be no time for celebrations. The buck continued climbing, his body awash with sweat, muscles rippling impressively in his arms, sinews bulging in his neck. His determination showed in every line of his face. So strong, so dangerous. Letting out an involuntary whimper, Dixon rolled onto the ledge and hastily slipped off the musket. He worked frantically, pouring in powder and ball, using the ramrod as best he could, his remaining fingers making heavy work of it. A trained soldier, under pressure of attack, could still fire off three shots in a minute. But Dixon was no trained soldier, plus his injury handicapped him considerably. Swearing as he fumbled to place more powder in the priming pan, the sweat dripped into his eyes, forcing him to rake the back of one trembling hand across his face.

Those vital seconds may have cost him his life.

The Indian came over the rim of the ledge, teeth clenched in his wild, bronzed face. Dixon swung a kick, cracking his boot against the side of the young warrior's face. The buck yelped, lost his grip on the rock edge and slithered down.

But not far enough.

Peering over the lip, Dixon saw him clinging on, desperately trying to find another hold. For a moment their eyes locked onto one another and Dixon brought up the musket and fired.

They heard the shot echoing between the soaring sides of the rocks as they squatted next to the dead bodies.

Two men, dressed in buckskins, their hair wild, faces burned almost black by the fierce sun, their skin like leather. Both stopped, exchanging bewildered looks and instinctively went into a crouch.

They lured the pair of soldiers into this lonely place, having feigned ignorance of their approach, swooping on them without sound or warning, slitting throats, hacking off the tops of their skulls. There were two others somewhere, but they would have to wait.

And then came the gunshot.

Both armed with muskets, a pair of pistols in their belts and long, twin-edged knives at their sides, neither spoke, their eyes roaming the rock summits. Hunters, their skills honed to perfection, they both understood the dangers such a place held if an attack came. So they sat and waited, readying themselves for an assault.

On the far side of the buttes, well out of sight of the two hunters, Dixon cursed. His shot shaved the side of the young warrior's head. Luckily for his target, the warrior had veered away when his foot slipped again, the bullet grazing his skull, leaving a long red welt across his right temple area. If anything, this slight wound spurred him onto greater efforts and, spouting a series of Native oaths and curses, he set about climbing once more.

Dixon, knowing he did not have the time to load up another shot, whirled around, craning his neck to look upwards. The rock face appeared sheer, with little possibility of escape. Over to his left, where the ledge seemed to curl around the rock, there might be some possibility of escape via another route. He edged slowly across, flattening himself against the face, the ledge a slender half-pace wide.

Closer now to the side, he looked around and gasped.

A pathway of sorts, either natural or cut out by people aeons ago, ran some forty feet or so to the valley below. Elated, he hunched his shoulders and readied himself to set off in a mad dash.

He took a breath and went to move forward.

The arrow struck him in the left shoulder.

The sudden unexpectedness of the blow caused him to lose his balance and stumble. Throwing out his arms in a wild, desperate bid to save himself, he pitched forward onto the narrow path and rolled down in a mad, uncontrolled tumble which sent him over the edge and into midair.

Waiting, breath bated, the two hunters watched as the body hit the hard ground, legs kicking out, the arrow snapped off, point protruding from just beside the bicep.

The man writhed and moaned, but he was alive.

"What the fuck?" asked the buckskin-clad hunter closest to the stricken stranger.

"There," said his companion, pointing upwards.

A young warrior stood, nocking a second arrow.

"To hell with this," said the first, bringing up his long-barrelled musket and firing. The shot hit the warrior in the chest. He tottered backwards, bow falling from his lifeless hands, legs working from pure nervous instinct before they buckled and he crumpled forward, falling down to hit the dirt with a tremendous slap.

"We gotta move fast."

And they did, breaking cover and running towards the two bodies.

"This one's leaner," said the killer, prodding the dead warrior with a thick finger. "We'll take him."

"And the other one?"

"Leave him, together with the soldiers. The buzzards will pick 'em all clean soon enough."

Laughing, the killer draped the dead warrior over his huge shoulders and the two hunters scurried away, disappearing along a narrow pathway which cut through the imposing rocks.

Dixon lay on his back, every bone creaking, every muscle ruptured, and turned his head to see two buckskin-clad men running away. He wanted to call after them, to plead for their help, take him with them, but he did not have the strength. So he remained still, peering up towards the sky and giving a strangled cry when he caught sight of the first bird soaring majestically across the unsullied blue.

The pain rode over his body like a living thing, an uncontrolled stampede of relentless agony.

And then he slipped into thankful unconsciousness.

Ten

Climbing up onto the back of his pinto pony, Deep Water grimaced and reached out to rub his leg. A quick glance towards Simms spoke volumes.

The detective frowned. "That old wound still giving you pain?"

"Discomfort only," said the scout dismissively, quickly pointing out across the prairie. "The war-party veer away to the east, but the men you seek take the opposite route."

"That'll work in our favour."

"Hopefully." The scout kicked his pony into a gentle walk. "Their steps grow more twisted."

"Twisted?" Simms moved his horse up alongside his friend as they cut across the open range.

"If that is the word. Like they are tiring, moving more slowly, with more effort."

"Only to be expected, out here in the open, on foot. It's a wonder they got this far."

"Something made the war-party move away. There were other tracks. Perhaps a scout returning to tell them news."

"Well, whatever it is that took 'em away, it means we can put all our attention into apprehending our boys." Instinctively he pulled out the Colt Navy and checked the load. After that, he went through the same routine with the Smith and Wesson. "Whatever state they're in, I doubt they will come quietly."

"What is it they have done?"

"Something to do with some Senator out East, making his way across to Salt Lake to help with the negotiations with Brigham Young."

"They killed him?"

Simms shrugged, slipping the Smith and Wesson back into his shoulder holster. "Beats me. I am not privy to the details and the telegram didn't go into the details. All I do know is they broke out of prison and made their way across the Territory. No doubt they'll tell us when we catch up with 'em."

"You think it will be that easy?"

"They is a bunch of killers, old friend – there'll be nothing easy about any of this, believe you me."

For the rest of that afternoon, they plodded on, their backs bowed against the baking sun, not even pausing to take water from their canteens. With little or no shade, the barren plains stretching endlessly in all directions, they had no choice but to continue. Simms himself could barely see the signs of the men. To him, whenever he did fasten on something different in the ground, they were not much more than scuffed imprints, but to Deep Water he knew exactly what they meant. "They are desperate for water now. See how they stumble."

Simms couldn't, but he grunted in agreement.

Ahead, a range of jagged rocks broke up the bland, barren landscape and, without a word, Deep Water turned his pony towards them.

"They camped here," he said, dropping down to the ground beneath the shadow of the nearest rock. He picked his way through the cold ashes of an old fire and brought up a sliver of bone between thumb and forefinger. "They ate."

"There's little game around here," said Simms, casting his eyes across the prairie. "Maybe a buck-rabbit or somesuch."

Deep Water climbed onto the back of his pony. "They then passed onto the far side."

They followed the trail and eventually came to a steep ridge. From here, they had an uninterrupted view across the plain, which from this point changed its complexion, with many more outcrops of rock, scrub and even several woody glades giving more variety to the vista.

Amongst it were the remains of a covered wagon.

The scout turned to his friend. "The horse, or horses, have gone."

"Could be Indians?"

"Maybe."

Deep Water kicked the pony's flank and soon both men were descending the rutted, winding trail towards the remnants of the wagon. Some distance away, Simms reined in and drew out his Root rifle. "I'll cover you."

The scout grunted and dismounted, moving across the ground in a whisper, keeping low.

Simms watched, occasionally allowing his eyes to roam across the land. The trees bothered him. Watchers may be lurking inside, and with the closest copse less than one hundred paces away, anyone with a musket could take a good shot.

He considered exploring the shaded depths, but then Deep Water was next to him again, breathing hard.

"Remember you told me about that Tabatha woman, what her family did to those others out on the trail?"

Simms's guts tightened. "Jesus. Cannibals?"

A slight nod. "They came upon them quickly. There is blood, signs of a struggle. Maybe three, four people died here. But ... " He turned away for a moment, a trembling hand wiping away moisture from his lips. "There is nothing left of them. I guess these men, they took the bodies to another place to dismember and cook them."

"The camp. That bone?"

Deep Water swung up onto the back of his pony, his features set hard. "They say the eating of your own kind changes you. Turns you into something not human."

"Well, if Tabatha was anything to go by that is true enough – she was a murdering bitch. I have never relished killing, Deep Water, but I feel the world is a mite safer without her in it."

"Even though White Dove killed her?"

Simms blinked, remembering the moment at Twin Buttes when Tabatha had the drop on him, and White Dove's bullets tearing into her, ending her miserable existence there and then. "Yes," he said, voice heavy, "she killed her. And I'm grateful for it."

"These men, if they too have changed because of what they have done ..."

He left the sentence unfinished, his eyes penetrating into Simms's own. The detective motioned to the nearby trees with his rifle. "We should take a look, see where it goes."

"You are becoming skilful, my friend."

"How do you mean?"

The scout grinned, "Because that is exactly where their footsteps lead."

Eleven

"I do declare," said Brewster, considering the hunk of dripping flesh in his hand, cooked on the hearth to what he believed to be perfection, "I enjoy female meat more than I do the male."

Curly munched on his own portions in silence. They sat on the floor in front of the flames and Curly, having found an old dust sheet in one of the other rooms, laid it down and had done his best to present something of a banquet for them both with plates and cutlery and some chipped cups for their water. He gave Brewster a meaningful look. "I couldn't have cut Arthur up anyway."

"No, I wasn't meaning him – Jesus, Curly. No. I don't believe I could have eaten our old friend, not even if we were close to starving."

With a sudden violent jerk of the arm, Curly hurled his piece of meat into the fire and watched it spit and sizzle. "I ain't got the stomach for any of this anymore."

Pausing in the act of taking another bite, Brewster sighed. "Curly, it's not as if we have any choice. We have one shotgun and a scalping knife between us. Even if there were anything to hunt, it's likely we would fail. Our situation forces us to do these things. If we didn't, we'd die."

"Even so, I ain't doing it no more."

"And risk dying?"

"If needs be." He held his stomach, face creasing up. "I don't feel too good."

"Hell, Curly, that is your *mind* telling your guts to reject what you've only just eaten. She would have killed us."

"Yes. I know that."

"Well then. You have nothing to feel guilty about."

"Don't I? Don't you remember those poor bastards we killed out on the range? How they squealed. They was nothing but peaceful pilgrims, Brewster."

"Luck would have it a band of savages would have done for them anyway."

"They had one goddamned mule, Brewster. Indians don't take mules. They would have left them be."

"You don't know that."

A distant look came into Curly's eyes and his voice dropped when he said, "What I know is, we killed 'em. And we ate them. And I reckon we is damned because of what we done, Brewster." Another groan and, cramped up, he swung away and vomited violently onto the floor.

"Ah shit," said Brewster and tossed his own unfinished morsel into the fire. "Now you've made me lose my goddamned appetite."

"You're all heart, ain't you, Brewster." Curly sat up, took up the front end of his shirt and wiped the sweat from his face with it. "I feel like shit."

"You look like shit."

His lips formed into a thin liner. "Brewster, if you don't—"

He froze, face aghast, eyes staring out through the open door.

"What the hell is it?"

Curly brought his finger to his lips, then gestured for Brewster to move away. "Get behind the door," he whispered, "with as little noise as you can." His eyes snapped towards the shotgun propped up beside the hearth.

Brewster rolled across the floor without a word and flattened himself under the window adjacent to the open door. At the same time, Curly scooped up the shotgun and flattened himself on the floor, both barrels trained towards the entrance.

He saw them and knew they could not see him, the bright sunlight casting the house interior in darkness. There were two men nervously stepping out from the tree line. Dressed in buckskins, exactly as the girl was, they stopped and looked around before exchanging a word or two. One had a brown, naked body draped over his massive shoulders. Both men appeared dirty and unkempt, their great shocks of tangled, matted hair giving them a wild, unnerving look. And both were armed.

"Bethany," shouted the closest man suddenly.

The single name rang out loud and clear, like the peel of a doom-laden bell announcing the death of someone.

Easing the corpse to the ground, the second man swung his musket from his shoulder. Curly saw it, recognising it as an old piece, but accurate enough to blow a hole through his head from such a close distance. He heard the ominous click of the hammer drawing back. The closest man repeated the action of his friend. Two muskets, two shots, but Curly saw too the revolvers stuck in their belts. Odds were not in his favour.

"*Bethany*," the man shouted again, his voice edged with obvious anxiety.

The seconds dragged by and the two men stood, motionless, heads titled slightly, listening. Curly blinked as a tear of sweat dropped from his eyebrow. He caught Brewster's terrified look and brought up his palm. "*Wait*," he mouthed.

The closest man breathed, "Something ain't right. She should be here."

"Take a look inside, Tomas. I'll scoot around back."

Tomas. Eyes locked on the open door of the house, raised an index finger and waggled it towards an area of ground a pace or two ahead of him. "There is blood here, Isaiah."

"Shit."

"Maybe they have gone, whoever they were."

"And taken Bethany? I'll skin them alive if they have."

Looking around, Tomas dropped down to his haunches and searched for more signs. After a few seconds, he shook his head. "No signs they moved away, leastways not far. I get the sense bodies were dragged across the earth and there are footsteps leading right to the door." He grunted. "The blood is dry but there was a lot of it. And shotgun pellets too." Too give weight to his discovery, he scooped up a small pile of lead and studied the pieces for a moment or two before allowing them to filter back through his open fingers.

Isaiah snapped his head towards his companion. "They must be from her shotgun, which means she is still here." He took a deep breath. "*Bethany!*" he roared.

They waited.

Across the room of the house, Brewster threw out his hands, mouth gaping, "*What is happening?*"

Again, Curly's palm remained still, mouthing again, "*Wait.*"

"Maybe she's out back," said the one called Tomas as he stood up.

"She'd have heard me calling by now."

"Then what do we do?"

"You wait here whilst I take a look."

Curly's hand came slowly down, finger wrapping around the trigger of his gun.

Isaiah, going into a low crouch, moved cautiously forward, eyes darting left and right, and when he stepped up onto the front porch, the ancient timbers groaned under his weight. A moment's pause. He was one pace away from the entrance.

"*Now,*" screamed Curly, and Brewster moved, like the expert he was, diving headfirst into the midsection of the gigantic man on the porch, hurling him down onto the ground, where he pinned him, the knife already sinking through the buckskin and penetrating the flesh.

Curly ran out, discharging both barrels at the second man who, despite his surprise, managed to loose off a shot from the musket. The ball smacked into the doorframe next to Curly's head.

But his blast did its work, throwing the man backwards, where he writhed and screamed.

Ignoring Brewster's struggle with the first Wildman, Curly stepped down, breaking open the shotgun, and fed in the last two remaining cartridges.

His casual approach proved his undoing.

The second Wildman, the one called Tomas, sat up, the Navy Colt in his hand, and his first bullet streaked past Curly's shoulder in a red arc. The second hit him in the shoulder.

"Damned bastard."

It was Brewster. He strode past Curly, who fell to his knees, clutching at the wound, and kicked Tomas under the chin. As the blow propelled the big man backwards, Brewster moved in fast, plunging the knife three times into the stricken man's throat then stepped back to admire his handiwork.

The only sounds were the gurgling of the two Wildmen, desperate to stem the frothing blood gouting from their destroyed throats. Brewster grinned, brandishing the Navy. "Seems we have procured ourselves the mean to salvation."

"I don't think so," said Curly, eyes screwed up, hand clamped to his shoulder.

"Ah shit, Curly, you've had worse than that. You saved me, I'll save you."

"I hope you do, old friend. But I tell you this – you had better work quick. This thing inside me will kill me just as sure as there is the sun in the sky."

"Then I'll get right to it," said Brewster, wiping the blade of his knife on the buckskin trouser leg of his dying victim, whose thrashing and moaning were growing less.

Curly watched his friend's approach and wondered if it might just as soon bleed out than suffer his butchering.

Twelve

Six months before, and three days out from Fort Laramie, a stagecoach trundled along the rutted trail, heralding its passage by the loud, grating clinking and clanking of axles and the motion of the thorough-brace, which sent everything topside into a frenzy, the railings barely able to save the luggage and other items from falling to the ground.

Inside the sweltering coach, Senator Bowen sat squeezed between his aide, Withers, and a large woman dressed in prim blue dress and pillbox hat. Opposite, on the other seat, two businessmen clutched satchel bags balanced on their knees, looking green with travel-sickness. Crushed up against the side window was another man, lean, three-day's worth of stubble on his hard chin, Navy Colt revolver in his waistband.

"How far is it now, Withers?"

The aide looked askance at his boss. "I'll check." He leaned his thin frame out of the window to shout topside, "How far?"

The guard beside the driver grunted, craning his neck. He frowned. "Hell, mister. How should I know?"

"Well, you is driving this damned crate."

"No I ain't." The guard grunted again and said to the driver. "How much further, Drake?"

Drake shouted, "Three, maybe four hours. Hard to tell, Clem, as the state of the trail is playing merry hell with my wheels so I have to take care. If I go any faster, we're bound to break an axle."

Clem relayed this news to Withers who struggled back into his seat, breathing hard with the exertion. "I don't like this damned heat," he said to no one in particular.

"We have to make Laramie before nightfall," said Bowen. "We have to set out across the plain to make it to Salt Lake City. My appointment with Brigham Young won't wait."

Withers acknowledged the Senator's concern by reaching into his coat and pulling out a slim, black leather bound diary. He opened it, licking his finger to turn the pages. "The President has set up the meeting for the day after tomorrow, sir."

"Hmm ... well, I prefer to be early."

"Yes, I do understand, but there is no need for panic, sir, we are well on schedule to—"

"Don't you lecture me, damn you," the Senator said, snapping his head around, glaring at his aide. "If I say we must be there a day before, we will be there a day before."

"Yes, sir." Withers closed his book, went to put it back in his pocket and caught the sneer from the lean man opposite. Twisting away, feeling distinctly uncomfortable, Withers ran a finger under his collar and peered out. "It never gets this hot in Chicago."

"I have known it to be so hot," commented the woman in the pillbox hat, "that I have seen horses fall down dead in the street from heatstroke."

"Dear Lord," said Withers.

"Forgive me, kind lady," said Senator Bowen, unconsciously doffing the hat he did not wear, "I am sure that must be an exaggeration."

"I have seen it with my own eyes, sir," she said, her cheeks growing a slight pink colour.

"I have seen steers dropping dead out on the range," put in the lean man with the Navy Colt. "Summers here can be hotter than hell."

Bowen gave the man a look like he might do to a young, naive child. "Hell, like most things to do with religious teachings, is a mere fantasy, created to instil fear in the masses and ensure their obedience. It does not exist, and certainly not in the bowels of this good earth."

The lean man frowned at the Senator. "Well, perhaps when the good Lord made Colorado, he plonked Hell right here."

"I do not know Colorado," said Bowen, turning away from the frown. "Nor Utah. These remain, for the most part, uncharted lands. Anything is possible, I guess."

"You're damned right," said the man and glanced out of the window. "Anything *is* possible."

Up top, Clem removed his hat and dragged the back of his forearm across his brow. He reached down and lifted up a canteen, unstopping the cork cap and drinking fitfully. Gasping, he offered it to Drake who shook his head once, keeping his eyes locked ahead.

Glancing around, Clem considered the sprawl of iron-grey earth stretching in all directions, punctuated with withered scrub and distant, soaring mountains. This area was not as dangerous as most and, when the railroad finally cut through this barren land, civilisation would at last arrive. It would mean the end of the stage, of course, and his job with it, but he was looking to retire within the year.

He repositioned his hat and thought he saw something. A plume of dust or smoke, coming from out of what must have been a elongated dip in the ground. He squinted, trying to make out what caused it. A sudden squall, a stampede of buffalo or deer, perhaps a rider. But what would a rider be doing all the way out here? Unless… He checked the shotgun, snapping it closed again with resolute force. Instinctively, he then checked the Paterson at his hip. He needed a carbine. On his next trip, he'd purchase one, charge it to the company.

Drake, noticing Clem's preparations, shot him a worried glance. "What's got you so jittery?"

"Might be nothing," said Clem, keeping his eye on the dust. The brown and grey cloud appeared to be growing. "Might be Bannocks."

"Shit, this far east?" Drake gently hauled back on the reins, slowing the team down slightly. "If they have horses, we won't be able to outrun 'em."

"What do you propose, make a stand here?"

"If it's Bannocks, they will want the horses, not a fight. If we pick off one or two, they'll give it up soon enough." He turned and peered into the distance. He hissed sharply. "It *is* horses, goddamned it."

"Could be anyone."

"Yeah, and it *could* be Bannocks. I'll pull up and we'll shoot the bastards before they can do any harm."

"And if it's just pilgrims or the like?"

"Then we'll continue on our way, but I ain't taking no chances, Clem."

Clem sniffed and turned to answer his colleague when he saw something beyond Drake's shoulder. "Oh my dear God."

The first bullet hit Drake high up on the left arm. He squealed, dropping the reins, right hand clamping over the wound; the horses went into hysterics, battling against their harness, jerking the stage forward. Panicking, Clem leaned across and hauled in on the reins, struggling to bring the horses to a halt. Gritting his teeth, he tried to engage the break by his side, but in so doing managed to cause the shotgun to slide from his lap and go clattering to the ground.

"Oh sweet Jesus," he breathed, straining to pull on the reins with one hand, the brake on the other. Beside him, Drake was crying with the pain, his face suddenly ghostly white.

The second bullet hit the driver in the throat, snapping back his head, and he threw up both hands to claw at the debilitating wound. He half-rose from his seat, lost his balance and pitched forward between the still galloping horses.

Screeching out every oath he knew, Clem let go of the brake, took the reins in both hands and, pressing his feet down hard, he straightened his back, virtually standing up. With all his considerable strength, he brought the team to a final halt.

Inside the coach, turmoil erupted.

With the first shot, the woman screamed, "Indians!" whilst the two businessmen exchanged glances and furiously unfastened their satchels. Bowen, pressing himself back in his seat, keeping his body as far away from the open windows as he could, whimpered, "Holy shit, what in the name of hell is going on Withers?"

But Withers wasn't listening. He was too busy peering through the open side window towards the fast approaching riders thundering over the plain. His moment of relief at them not being Indians soon drained away when he saw the raised revolvers in their hands and the bandanas across their faces. "We're being robbed," he breathed.

"Like hell we are," said the lean man opposite, pulling out the Navy from his waistband and checking it.

The two businessmen each now sported Colt's Revolving Pocket Pistols. Bowen gazed at them in horror, "What is this? Are you two...?"

They both smiled. The one to the right put the muzzle of his pistol against the lean man's head and said, "Put the fucking gun down."

The man did so without a word, eyeing Bowen as if apologising for not realising sooner the two men were in league with the robbers.

"Oh God," moaned Withers.

"Shut up," said the one on the left. The woman opposite made no sound, not since her initial scream, and pressed a clean, white hand-kerchief against her mouth. "You're pretty."

Bowen leaned forward, angry. "Now you just listen here, if you think we—"

The man swung his revolver around and smacked it hard against the side of Bowen's head. Clutching at his face with both hands, blood seeping between his fingers, he fell against Withers.

"Have you any ideas who this is?" squealed the aide.

"He better be rich," leered the assailant, and looked again at the woman. "What's your name, honey?"

"Cut it out Roscoe, we're not here for frilly knickers and smooching on the back-lawn. You," he thrust his gun straight towards Withers, "when this crate comes to a complete halt, you get out, keep the door open and don't do anything I don't tell you to do."

"Yes, sir."

Leaning forward, the man scooped up the Navy Colt from the floor. "I'll be taking this first."

They all lurched as the stage came to a sudden halt, Bowen and the woman thrown forward towards the two men. Withers, gripping the window frame, remained rooted to his seat and the lean man took his chance, turned and punched the man next to him across the jaw.

From then on, things turned nasty.

Curly reined in his horse and studied the man on the top as he struggled in reaching down between the panting, nervous team of horses to retrieve his shotgun.

Turning to spit into the ground, Curly pulled out his revolver and shot the guard in the neck.

"Shit, we weren't supposed to kill nobody," said Brewster, coming up alongside him, horse snorting, its eyes wild with terror at the sudden gunshot.

"Well, nothing ever goes to plan does it?" Curly pointed towards the other riders coming up fast on the opposite side of the stage. "Tell them to pull down the money chest. We're here to make this look like a robbery, remember." He dismounted and stooped down to peer amongst the stomping hooves of the horses. He sighed. "Bastard ain't dead."

"Leave him," said Brewster, leading his horse around the back of the stage to meet up with the others.

Curly grunted, chewing his lip. "He sure does bleed a lot."

Pricking his ears to some altercation coming from the interior of the stage, he eased back the hammer of his revolver and stood up, listening intensely.

After a moment, he stepped to his side and, perhaps no more than six feet from the closed door of the stage, put three shots into the coach.

In a blur, the lean man caught the other man's wrist, twisting it to the side with a vicious yank and striking him a tremendous blow across the jaw. The man crumpled, as his partner had before him. The lean man caught the small Colt before it dropped and shot a look towards Bowen and Withers. "You stay here and stay low."

The woman cried out, imploring with both hands, "Dear God Almighty, you can't leave us alone with them!"

The lean man glanced towards the two moaning businessmen sprawled across the bench seat, and smiled. He picked up the Navy and handed her one of the small Colts. "You cover 'em. If they try to move, but a bullet in 'em."

He turned to go, to face the riders fast approaching from across the prairie.

Three bullets tore through the coach, hitting him in the back, blasting him through the very door he was about to open, dumping him into the dirt beyond.

The woman screamed. Bowen clung onto Withers as a wide-eyed, sweat-stained, grime-infested individual stuck his head through the open side window. He took one look at the sight greeting him and shook his head.

"Which one of you is Senator Bowen?"

"I am."

"Good to know you. General Winstanley sends his regards."

"General who?"

"Winstanley. Mormon field commander." He winked, brought up his revolver and shot Bowen in the head.

Thirteen

"Two hours. No more." Deep Water rubbed the soil between forefinger and thumb, sniffing at the baked blood.

"Seems like they had a real set-to," said Simms, eyes roaming across the three dead bodies, two out in the open, the third half-in, half-out of the house.

"This one," said Deep Water, prodding the corpse nearest to him, "is one of the war-party we shadowed."

"How in the hell did he get here?"

"I do not know. Perhaps we will never know. But we must move fast, in case the others come looking."

Simms snorted and climbed into his saddle. "I could have done with a few moments, get a better sense of what went on here, but I know you're right – let's move on."

Deep Water led the way, skirting the tree line of the small wood until eventually they moved out into open ground again. From this point they broke into an easy canter, aware their mounts were close to exhaustion. They required watering and rest but the thought of their pursuers gaining on them meant they needed to maintain momentum. So they rode, as gently as they dared.

At some point in the early evening, as the sun slowly dropped beneath the horizon, giving some respite to the intense heat, Deep Water hauled in his reins and waited. Simms, some distance behind, came up alongside, breathing hard, pausing only to mop his face with his neckerchief.

"What is it?"

"There," said the scout, his finger pointing into the distance.

"Well, I'll be damned," snarled Simms.

He noticed a small smudge, nothing more than a dark stain on the rolling plain and quickly pulled out his field glasses and set them to his eyes.

It was them. Two men, riding on the back of a large, gangly mule. Even from this distance, they appeared exhausted, the poor animal doing its best, legs plodding heavily.

"Can you shoot them?"

"Not from this distance," breathed Simms, putting the glasses into their case. "But by the look of them, we'll overtake them within the hour."

Looking over to the west, Deep Water sighed. "We have less than an hour of daylight. It will be touch and go."

"They'll make a fire."

"They cannot be so stupid."

Chuckling, Simms readjusted himself on the saddle, stretching up from the stirrups. "Don't count on it."

In the cold chill of the open plain, Brewster set to making a small fire. By now he was well versed in such a task, using his knife and a piece of flint to set sparks to bunches of coarse, dry bracken. He fed the burgeoning flames with small pieces of kindling until, in little over ten minutes, the fire took hold and he dropped on larger hunks of wood. "This place is tinder dry," he said, turning his knife in the flames.

"Brewster, do you know what you're doing with that goddamned knife?"

Brewster swivelled on his haunches. In the eerie half-light between dusk and night, he could clearly see the deathly pallor spreading over his friend's features. "You need to bite down on something," he said and chose one of the small, gnarled twigs on the ground next to him.

Shuffling across to his friend, he placed the twig into Curly's mouth. "This is going to hurt, Curly, but I have to get that lead out. You'll die if I don't."

Curly grunted, squeezing his eyes closed. "Just do it, damn you." Then he bit down on the twig.

Brewster deftly cut away Curly's shirt. He held up the knife and studied the blade and was about to cut into the purple and red wound when something moved behind him. He whirled around.

"Take it easy," said the man, tall and slim, emerging from the shadows. hat masking his features, right hand by his side, gun in hand pointing unerringly towards Brewster, who whimpered.

Another man, an Indian, moved up close and dropped to his knees next to Curly. He inspected the wound and after a moment turned his face to Brewster. "You are lucky," he said, taking the knife away from him with almost reverential care. "Hold him by the shoulders, with all your strength."

And then he set to work.

Simms dozed intermittently through the night, swapping guard with Deep Water every few hours. Curly, alive with fever, rolled and cursed under his blanket, his body awash with sweat but Brewster, oblivious to it all, slept as a baby, the only difference being his grinding snores which set Simms's teeth on edge and made staying awake easier.

At one point, Curly sat bolt upright, eyes white in his face, yelling, "She's here – take her away from me, Christ! Oh Christ!"

He crumpled back into troubled sleep and Deep Water, mopping his brow, tutted, "He is close to death."

"We have to keep him alive. They want him fit for hanging."

"We can only hope."

"Yep," drawled Simms and settled back against his rock, "I guess that is all we will ever have."

Fourteen

Fort Bridger hummed with the sound of clattering wagons, the neighing and snorting of horses and the gaggle of voices from a hundred different lands. Leaning against a post outside his office, Major Porter eyed the entire scene with a sense of detached amusement.

"Never have been able to fathom out the attraction," he said.

"What's that, sir?" asked the young lieutenant standing a little way behind.

"All these pilgrims heading out west. I thought once the Goldrush ended, all of this nonsense would too. There ain't nothing out there but scrub, dried up river beds and bloodthirsty Redskins."

"Have you ever been out west, sir?"

Porter turned a brooding eye on the young officer. "What does that mean, boy?"

"Just wondering, sir – nothing more."

"Have you?"

"Er, yes I have sir. My uncle led a detachment into New Mexico just after the Mexican War, sir. He liked it so much, he settled there, and my father soon joined him."

"Happy families, was it?"

"Not at all, sir. My mother contracted fever and was dead within a month. My two older sisters both died giving birth and my brother, Nate, went off somewhere to earn his fortune in California. Never heard nor seen of him again. I was not more than five by the time this all happened, sir."

"Jesus." Porter turned away. He pulled out a thin box of cigars, chose one and chomped off the end. Without a word, the lieutenant reached over and put a match to the Major's smoke. Porter grunted, puffing on the cheroot and sent out a stream of smoke. Pointing with it, he continued, "See these families – they have no idea. They've been sold a lie. Look what happened to you. Damn tragedy, that's what that is."

"Well, I, er, don't rightly see it that way, sir. My father, you see, he re-married. Gwendoline was her name, and she was a wonderful woman. She raised me and we were as happy as anyone could hope to be."

"Despite all of your loss? Jeez, boy, you have sand, I'll give you that."

"My Uncle managed to procure me a commission in the Army, and here I am."

"What's your name, boy."

"Lieutenant Faulkner, sir."

"I know that – I meant your first name."

"Ah, it's, er, Orvis, sir.

"Orvis … All righty, Lieutenant Orvis, you ever come across those Mormons whilst out in New Mexico?"

"No, sir. But I have heard things. That they have many wives, and that they are friends with Indians."

"Did you hear it said they have reached agreements with the US Government?"

"A sort of truce, so I understand."

"Yeah, well. They sent a commissioner out to agree terms. Senator Bowen. He ended up dead. Did you hear about that?"

"It was in the papers. Six months or so ago."

"Ah ha." He puffed on his cigar. "They are sending a Federal agent to investigate. He's due here tomorrow."

"A Federal agent?"

"They have suspicions Bowen was deliberately killed – an assassi-nation. The stagecoach he was travelling in was held up, and he got shot. Probably trying to be a hero."

"No doubt." He shifted position. "I have heard and read such things, sir. The manner of the Senator's death. A single bullet in the head. It was no random shooting."

Porter grunted. "I want you to meet this Federal agent, Lieutenant. I want you to escort him out towards the trail." He again pointed with the cigar. "Most of these people will be heading the same way, so you won't be in any danger of being attacked. Show him the site where those varmints robbed the stage. I have a map."

"You have a map?" A tiny laugh. "Why would you have a map?"

"Because I am nothing but fastidious, Lieutenant." He swung around and prodded the young officer in the chest with the cigar butt. "You'd best remember that." He then pushed past the young officer and dipped into his office.

Faulkner stared at the disappearing back of his commander and wondered what he was supposed to show the visiting Federal agent exactly. The remnants of a broken stagecoach, maybe dried blood, a few spent pieces of lead? Not exactly earth-shattering evidence which was going to bring any new light on what happened or, perhaps more tellingly, why.

He pricked up his ears to the sound of voices raised in anger and, seeing a bunch of pilgrims squaring up to each other, he readjusted his belt and hat and sauntered over.

"What seems to be the problem here, folks?"

There were five or six men, red faces twisted in rage, jabbing fingers at one another. Two men on one side, the rest facing them. Uneven odds, as far as Faulkner could see.

"They took the grain," spat one of them.

"We did not," rebuked the other, one of the two men on the receiving end of so much anger.

"Hold on," said Faulkner, stepping in between them, holding up his hand. "Why not just tell me what this is all about?"

"*Grain!*" said the closest man, heavyset, red-haired and red-shirted. His fists bunched. "We was in the merchant store, buying provisions and what not, and we come on out and find these two helping themselves to our grain from the back of the wagon."

"We did not," said the other again, "that was our grain we was loading up. Ask the goddamned storekeeper if it isn't."

"Well our grain has gone," said another man, looking behind redshirt, "and you is the only ones here – so it must have been you!"

A new surge of shouting, jaw jutting forward, fists raised.

"Let's just see," said Faulkner, raising his voice above the tumult, "let's just see what the storekeeper has to say." He pointed to the wagon belonging to the two men. "They have three bags of grain from what I can see."

"We had six, goddamn it," said Red-shirt, turning to his own wagon. "We have but three left."

"Did you see 'em?"

Red-shirt frowned. "See what?"

"Did you see these gentlemen taking your grain from your wagon?"

A moment's silence, the exchanging a few questioning glances, "Well, we didn't actually *see* them, but there was no one else."

"Really?" Faulkner cast his eyes over to the large entrance doors to the Fort, and the hunched-up individual driving a small, open wagon out into the trail. On board were three sacks of grain. ""I reckon you should take a longer look over yonder."

Red-shirt frowned again, deep this time, and turned to where Faulkner was looking. "Holy shit," he roared and broke into a run, his companions swiftly following.

"Thank you, Lieutenant," said one of the other two, extending his hand. "Name is Richard Morris. This here is my good friend and neighbour, Jasper Philips. They were getting ready to beat us up."

"I reckon so," smiled Faulkner, pushing his hat back from his brow. "You folks heading west?"

"Yes. We are well-provisioned. We have two wagons and we have oxen. Both our families are eager to get on our way."

"We're going to take one of the trails which lead off from the Oregon Trail," put in Philips. "We've heard it is the safest route."

"Well, it's certainly the most used and best known. It's always best to travel with as many other emigrants and pilgrims as you can. Not all Indians are hostile, but some are. Many are starving. This prolonged drought has caused great hardship for virtually everyone."

"Our plan is to head across towards Salt Lake," said Morris.

"That's quite a way. Most people nowadays veer northwest a little, head across to California."

"We reckon that since a peace agreement has been signed in Utah, we might have a better chance of settling down. Besides, we're Mormons."

"Ah." Faulkner nodded towards the Fort entrance where another altercation was about to erupt. "Seems like I'm needed again. You take care, folks, and every good fortune to you."

Doffing his hat, Faulkner strolled over towards the entrance.

Half an hour later, with the small, hunched up man put in the stockade for a few days, Faulkner wrote up his report. It was short, and to the point, but one thing troubled him more than anything else. Perhaps it was illogical, and had no connection to what happened at the stage holdup all those months ago.

Those pilgrims were Mormons, and the Senator was setting out to broker the peace-deal between the religious group and the US Government. Coincidence, or something more.

His hand remained poised over his report as an uneasy feeling developed deep inside.

Fifteen

They were no more than half a day on the return journey to Fort Bridger when Curly fell off the back of the mule.

Deep Water went to him first and his face, when he turned to Simms, spoke volumes.

They buried him amongst the scrub, hoping the coyotes wouldn't dig him up.

Brewster, sitting in the shade of a large boulder, rocked himself gently, holding his knees close to his chest.

"I knew we was stupid to try and make it out here," he wailed, the tears cutting tiny rivulets through the grime clinging to his face.

Sighing, Simms walked over to his horse and fitted the spade back into its holder on the saddle and leaned against the animal, breathing hard. "It's too damned hot for any of this."

"Or maybe it is your age," added Deep Water, repositioning a few rocks on top of the burial mound. He chuckled and, still grinning, stood up. "How old are you now?"

"I've still got a few good years in me. Maybe more than you."

"Ha! I doubt it, White Man!"

They both laughed and then Simms, growing serious, shot Brewster a quick glance. "Why did you come out here anyway? You must have known it's as mean as hell out here."

Brewster's face came up and he sniffed loudly, wiping his nose on the cuff of his filthy shirt. "Curly said we could find 'rich pickings'.

Those were his words. I have them ingrained in my head." He gave emphasis to his words by tapping his skull with a filthy finger. "Said we could find old forgotten towns, rob some banks."

"So you was headin' out across the Territory in the hope of finding these places? Seems mighty hit and miss if you ask me."

"No, he said he knew somebody. In a town called Twin Buttes."

Simms went rigid, snapping his head towards Deep Water, who frowned. "Twin Buttes?" repeated the Indian scout.

"That's what he said," continued Brewster. "He had some old friend of his there – the sheriff. Man name of—"

"Silas," said Simms, finishing off Brewster's sentence.

"Yeah, that was him. Said he was an old friend of his."

"Well ain't that interesting," said Simms. He straightened himself up and sauntered across to where Brewster sat. "What else did he say?"

"Not much, just that Silas could point us in the right direction, help us with supplies, food and such."

"Did Curly say how he knew Silas?"

"No, only what I've said. Look, I ain't lyin' to you, or nothin'. There ain't no point me lying about any of it, is there – not with Curly dead, and me going back to face a hanging in prison."

Stooping closer, Simms regarded the prisoner keenly. "How did you break out?"

"Eh? How did we break out?" His eyes grew wide and he looked towards Deep Water and back again to Simms, perspiration breaking out across his forehead. "What do you mean?"

"Exactly what I say – *how did you break out of prison?*"

Breathing became laboured, mouth trembled. "I ain't – shit, I don't know. We just did, that is all."

Simms tiled his head. "What, you just walked out of there, like you was leaving church or something?"

"Yeah, yeah that's it. We just walked out."

"I don't believe you."

Brewster pushed himself back hard against the rock. "Look, mister, you ain't got no call to be questioning me like this. I am in deep anxiety, what with me facing the gallows and all."

"I just want to know how it happened, that's all."

"Well, it ain't got nothing to do with you, now has it? Hell, I don't even have to talk to you."

"No, that's right, you haven't. But, let me put something to you. Ruminate on it a little while."

"Ruminate? What in hell does that—"

"Your good friend, poor old Curly, he died from that wound, all festering away, eating him alive … Now, there ain't no one out here to testify what exactly happened."

"What?" He laughed. "You telling me you're gonna pin all of that on me? What the hell – you can do what you like. They can't hang me twice, you piece of shit."

"No, that's true. But who said anything about hanging?" Simms smiled. "What I mean here is, my friend the Indian, he can do things to you which will make your eyes bleed."

Brewster snapped his head towards the scout. His voice quaked, "What in the hell do you mean?"

"I mean, he can split your tongue, pull out you intestines, stake you out in the sun and leave you here to fry – that's if the buzzards and the coyotes don't come and finish you off first."

"You – you wouldn't such a thing."

"Why not? Makes no difference to me." He gestured towards Deep Water, who pulled out a heavy-bladed knife from its sheath at his hip. "We can start right now … Unless you tell me all about it."

"Oh sweet Jesus. You wouldn't – you *can't*."

"Who will ever know," said Deep Water, running his thumb along the blade. When he brought his hand up for Brewster to see, the digit bled. "I enjoy seeing people die, especially people like you, you bloodsucking White bastard."

Brewster went to get up, but Simms put his fist against the man's chest and pushed him back. "Just tell it."

Brewster looked and whimpered.
His body sank into itself and he released a rattling sigh.
And then he told Simms everything he wanted to know.

Sixteen

"We hit the stage from both sides," Brewster said at the start of his story. "Curly and me, we came from the west side. Curly, he was a deadeye with that gun – any gun. He shot the driver, then did for the shotgun guard. I watched him walk up to the stage and shoot through the door. I think he hit some fella, who fell out on the other side. Then Curly walked up to the window and asked if there was a man named Bowen inside. I heard some voices, then Curly fired one more shot.

"The boys from the other side, they came riding in, hollerin' and a-shootin'. Arthur, he was there and when they got to the stage, they got the people out. We had two men working inside, dressed as businessmen, but they were in a bad way – they said the big, lean guy who Curly shot through the door punched 'em both clean out. We laughed at that.

"There was a woman. Some of the others, they took her away a piece. I heard her screamin', but I didn't do nothin' to her, I swear to God. Curly did, but Curly was like that. He took what he wanted. We all called him 'Lonseome' because he had no friends – he didn't trust anyone. We were all afraid of Curly.

"There was one guy in the stage, a little fella. He was tellin' us all how we would all hang for what we did to the Senator. Curly shot him, right through the head. Didn't miss a heartbeat in doing it. Just brought up his gun and *BAM*, that was the end of it. They all died in that stage ... 'cept of course, the big lean one. He looked dead, but he wasn't. After we had gone, so we discovered, he got up and walked all the way to the next staging station and told 'em what had happened. Next thing, a troop of cavalry came out of Fort Laramie to hunt us down.

"They caught us not far from a town called Fairweather. That was where we was headin'. We had the cash box and whatever else we could take from the bodies and we was plannin' on sharing it, but Curly, he said he wasn't interested. We were holed up amongst some buttes and made a fight of it, but them soldier boys were determined to shoot us all to hell. Four of us died, leaving me, Arthur and Curly. They then took us away and that was that."

Simms, who sat on the ground and listened to what Brewster said, rubbed his chin in contemplation for a moment. "Those two businessmen, how come they were in the stage?"

"Beats me. Curly, he did all the planning."

"And how did you meet Curly?"

"We go back a few years. Met back in Kansas in Fifty-Eight, I think it was. We were in a saloon, playing cards and got to talking. Well, we struck out west, robbed a bank or two, made some money. Late last year we travelled across to Laramie where we met up with some other boys before we rode on to Bridger. At the fort there, Curly, he would go and talk with some officer."

"Which officer?"

"Hell, I don't know – just some soldier, with bits of gold on his shoulder. In truth, it was the officer who came to us. He would meet up with Curly and then one morning, Curly tells us we are going to rob a stage. That suited us just fine, so off we set."

"So Curly knew when the stage was due?"

"He knew everything. Knew who would be on board, where it was headin', everything."

"You think this officer told him?"

"Beats me, but Curly never left that fort all the time we was there, so I guess someone must have given him all the details."

"And those businessmen? What was their part?"

"I have no idea, mister. They was on the stage when we held it up. To this day, I do not know who they were. And the soldiers killed 'em at the shootout so now no one will ever know."

Looking across to Deep Water, Simms motioned for the Indian to move away with him, out of Brewster's earshot.

"Clearly the whole holdup was a distraction, to kill the Senator. His killing was a deliberate assassination, no doubt about it."

"You think this officer in Bridger planned it all," said Deep Water, not looking too convinced. "What would be the reason?"

"I don't know. Bowen was on his way to negotiate the peace treaty. Maybe someone didn't want it to go ahead."

"But why? It serves no purpose to prolong the dispute."

"Unless someone has personal reasons to see the Senator dead. Maybe a grudge against Bowen, professional or political jealousy. Who knows."

"And then there is the way they escaped. Brewster, he seems to say they simply walked out."

"That can't be true. If it is, then they must have had inside help. And that means whoever is behind all of this wanted Curly free, but for what reason I don't know."

"Fear of him talking? If Curly was to make a deal with the authorities, tell them all about the plan and who was behind it …"

"You could be right. It makes more sense. Curly was going to hang anyway …" Grunting, Simms swung away and strode over to Brewster again. "You said you just walked out of that prison? Explain it to me."

"Well, we was cooped up, as we always was, when this particular mornin' the guards came along and told us we were to go out and help in one of the nearby cotton fields."

"Cotton fields? Was that usual?"

"No, not for us anyways. We had faced trail and were due to hang the following week. Maybe they was thinking we could spend our last few days out in the open air, enjoying a taste of freedom seeing as our days were numbered."

"So, you went off to the field, no questions asked?" Brewster merely shrugged. "Then what?"

"Well, the guards, they told us to team up with a group of negroes. So, that's what we did. Then Curly, he says the guards had gone."

Simms blinked. "Gone? Gone where?"

"I don't know. Them negroes, they was laughin' mighty loud, thought it was great fun. So we all skedaddled and here I am."

"You never once stopped to think it was strange, those guards just disappearing like that?"

"Hell, I wasn't about to hang around and ask 'em! We took our chance and got away. I took a knife from one of them black boys, but that was all we had. We had no way of knowing where we was head, 'cepting Curly had some idea to go over to Twin Buttes and meet up with that Silas fella. But I told you that, and there it is."

"And Curly never ever gave you any indication that somebody had helped you all to escape?"

"No sir, and we never asked. Curly was not the kind of man to press, if you get my meanin'. He was a hard, dangerous sonofabitch, and now he's dead. Arthur too. I am the only one left and I will be facing my maker soon enough."

Simms screwed up his mouth for a moment. "I could put in a word for you, Brewster. It might be too late to overturn the original judgement, but if there is anything else you can add it will do you no end of good. A name, for example."

Moving up alongside them, Deep Water loomed over them both. "The name of the officer at Bridger. You tell us, it will help."

"Might save you from hanging," agreed Simms. "You'd serve a term, maybe even life, but you'd still be alive."

Brewster's feverish eyes went from one to the other. "Hell, I can't remember…"

"Describe him."

"He – he was just like any other officer in the Army. Hell …" He screwed up his face as if in pain, even taking up massaging both his temples, agonising over the lack of recollecting the officer's name. "He had an office. Big man, never smiled, always looked as if he was having trouble with his shits."

"Constipated?"

"Is that the word? Hell, I don't know. He looked in pain."

"Pain? Serious?"

"A big man," said Deep Water. "Was his hair black or white?"

"I – I guess it was brown, but ..." Brewster's face came up, his eyes wide and bright, as if illuminated by a dozen or more candles. His right hand shot up and he snapped his fingers. "Hot dang, mister detective – I got it."

"Then tell us, you ignoramus, and save your miserable life!"

"It was Porter. Major-goddamned-Porter."

Seventeen

The wagons creaked and groaned, wheels jabbing into potholes, the ground rutted and iron-hard. Up on the driving board, Richard Morris struggled to prevent his pair of horses drifting from the trail. The sun beat down relentlessly. Upon his head, an old, beaten up straw hat kept most of the rays from searing into his brain, but his shirt, soaked in sweat, clung to his back, causing him to shift position, the discomfort like a second skin. The heat drained him, made him weary, forcing him to struggle in order to keep his eyes open.

Behind, inside the covered wagon, his wife Arabella peeled and diced vegetables, imaginatively preparing a range of stews from the meagre ingredients varied enough to satisfy everyone's appetite. Next to her, Millie, her fourteen-year-old daughter, helped as best she could, but the constant buffering and jolting of the wagon made working arduous and frustrating, the knife forever slipping, pieces of carrot and potato falling to the floor. "There's more out of the pot than in," she said and Arabella chuckled but added nothing.

Running beside the wagon with endless energy, laughing and enjoying themselves, were the two sons of the family – Jason and Castor. Their father, forever a lover of the Greek myths, chose their names. Arabella, on the other hand, would have no such classical meanings placed upon their only daughter's head. They were a cheery brood for the most part, resolute in their beliefs, and in their determination to cross the great plain and join their brethren at Salt Lake City.

A day out from Fort Bridger, their progress remained slow, Morris not wishing to push the horses too hard in the heat. In the early evening, he pulled in his team, jumped down and waved to Jasper in the second, trailing wagon, to slow down.

"There's a stream yonder, with tributaries and good pasture for the oxen. I reckon we camp there."

Jasper grunted, pushing back his hat from his forehead, his face baked nut brown by the sun. "I could do with resting up. We need water for ourselves as well as the animals."

"That's true enough," said Morris, pausing to look up at a sky of uniform blue. "I've never known heat like this."

"They say rain has not fallen for almost nine months."

"I can believe it." He blew out his cheeks, taking his cuff in his free hand and using it to wife his mouth. "Do you suppose it grows cold in the night? I have heard it said thus."

"It will be a welcome respite to this heat."

"Amen to that, old friend."

"We should keep guard. After the youngens are bedded down, one of us should stay awake." Jasper smiled. "I'll do the first few hours."

"God bless you for that, Jasper. I do not think I could stay awake much more than ten minutes."

They parted with a laugh and Morris, leading the little train towards the river, let out a whoop some thirty or forty minutes later when he spotted a cluster of three or more other wagons camped down in a glade.

A burly man in faded dungarees stepped out from the lengthening shadows of the trees. He held a carbine in a relaxed grip, his teeth shining white in his broad, cheerful face. He held up a beefy hand and Morris reined in his team. "Welcome strangers," the man said, his deep voice booming in the still of the evening, "Have you come far?"

"We left Fort Bridger more than a day since."

The man moved up to the nearest horse and patted its neck. "We ourselves came straight from Laramie. Have you come across anyone else?"

"No, not since leaving the Fort." Morris swivelled and gestured towards Jasper lumbering up behind. "There are two of us, families both. We are crossing towards Salt Lake."

"Well, the trail will take you there, but it becomes a mite difficult once you cross the border. Indians can be hostile, so it's best to have your wits about you." He patted the horse again, "My name is Jubal. Pass over yonder, friend, then come and join us for supper. We is four in our train, but new faces are always welcome."

Grinning his thanks, Morris flicked the reins and his wagon trundled on into the glade, making an easy route next to the river where he stopped. Jasper came up alongside, easing back on the reins. "All well?"

"All well," smiled Morris, and jumped down.

Soon the boys, both his own and Jasper's single son Rupert, were unhitching both teams and leading them off to drink. Jasper untied the oxen and watched the two enormous animals munch down the lush, succulent grass which sprouted in abundance this close to fresh water.

"They seem friendly enough," said Morris, stretching out his back with a groan.

"Apart from them unsavoury types back at the Fort, everyone we've met seems the same."

"I guess it is because we all share the same goal – to find a new life."

"No doubt. Whatever the truth of it, I cannot pretend I do feel much safer to be in the company of so many others."

"So far we have not encountered any semblance of trouble."

"We're only a day out, Richard. I overheard what that Jubal said regarding the border country. We need to be on our guard as we cross into Utah."

"But how will we know when we have crossed, Jasper? There ain't no signs."

"I'm guessing we will know well enough, my friend."

They joined the others after dusting themselves off, the girls trying to make themselves as presentable as possible, and soon they partook of beef broth served up in wooden bowls and strong coffee.

"We have heard many of the streams hereabouts carry disease," said one of the strangers, a thin-stick old man who spoke with a curious twang to his voice. He laughed at their expressions. "My name is Hammond. I'm a Scot, came over in Forty-Six, hoping to make it to Canada. Then the Goldrush came and I sort of got sidetracked."

"Ah yes. Gold. There were many fortunes made back in those days."

"Still are," said Jubal, sauntering up to join them. He sat down on a small rock and stretched out his hands towards the campfire. "Strikes are still being made and not all of them in California."

"I doubt any will ever be as big as those back in Forty-nine," said Hammond with feeling.

"Did you make anything?" asked Jasper.

The Scot cackled. "Well, I lost my wife and two children, as well as most of my teeth."

Jasper and Morris exchanged a look and turned to the Scot aghast, who laughed, causing their expressions to grow even more concerned.

"Boys, this is the way of this here country," said Hammond quickly, no doubt attempting to allay their fears. "After everything went pear-shaped, I returned to Kansas, settled down with a widow named Adeline but when she too died, I thought it best for me to strike out alone and head back to California once again. This life is nothing but eventful."

By the light of the fire, they continued swapping stories and at some point, as the moon appeared above the trees, someone produced a guitar and strummed a few chords. As the voices joined in song, Arabella's angelic voice pierced the night with her sweet tones and everyone grew silent, listening to the selection of hymns she sung.

Over the course of the next few days, they stayed with the group, bonds of friendship growing between them. And when it came time for them to part, the girls, having made good friends with some of the boys from the other families, shed tears and hoped they would all meet up again soon.

"They were good people," said Arabella, sitting next to her husband as he took their wagon onto the trail to the border which branched west from the main Oregon Trail.

"It would have prospered us all if they headed to Salt Lake."

"The Lord's path is the one we've chosen, Richard."

"It is, and it is the one we follow, in faith and in certainty."

On the fifth morning, Richard drew to a halt, shielding his eyes against the glare, the stark, barren land acting like a mirror reflecting the sunlight directly into his eyes. Coming up alongside, Jasper drew in his team and took a heavy breath. His wife had fashioned a crude form of veranda to keep him in shade as he drove. By now, however, his face glowed like burnished bronze, the creases around his eyes and mouth deep. "We cannot stop here, exposed as we are."

"No, it's not that," said Morris, pointing across the vast expanse of the plain. "We have company."

"Oh sweet Jesus," breathed Jasper.

Arabella appeared from inside the rear of the wagon. "What is it, why have we stopped?"

And then she saw them too, and a tiny moan of fear rattled from her throat.

Half a dozen Indians, astride sturdy pinto ponies, were moving with nonchalant ease directly towards them.

Eighteen

On the day the Federal agent arrived at Bridger, Faulkner was busy checking the condition of some horses, running his hand over their withers, shoulders, back and quarters. Lifting up each leg, he studied fetlocks, hocks and knees before paying particular attention to the hooves. Six horses in all, well rubbed down in preparation for a scouting patrol across country.

"You must be Faulkner."

The young lieutenant span around, hand instinctively moving towards the revolver at his hip. The newcomer came upon him so silently he almost cried out in alarm. He relaxed when he noted the man's calm exterior, grey beard fringing a solid looking jaw, ice-blue eyes looking out from a teak-coloured face, ingrained with hard lines across the brow. And his warm smile.

"Relax," said the man, stepping forward. He wore knee-length boots, grey pin-striped trousers and black frock coat, a tall black hat completing his attire. "Name is Cross. I'm the Federal agent from Washington you've been expecting."

Faulkner straightened up, feeling rather foolish at his overreaction. He forced a tight smile, patted the nearest horse on the neck and stepped forward, offering his hand. "Faulkner. Sorry about ... " He shrugged, looked away as he felt the heat rising to his cheeks. "I'm always on my guard where horses are concerned." He gestured towards the tethered animals, all of them growing tense, the atmosphere charged with apprehension. The heavy smell of straw and oats mingled with horse sweat to hit the back of the throat. Faulkner coughed and Cross took his hand. A firm handshake, strong. The Lieutenant looked into the man's cold eyes and realised this was no ordinary individual.

"I understand you will be accompanying me to the site of the holdup."

"Yes sir, that I shall." Dropping his hand, Faulkner unconsciously wiped his palm across the seat of his pants. "Sorry, I, er—"

"Quit apologising, Lieutenant. I spoke with your immediate superior. A Major Proctor?"

"*Porter*, sir."

"Yes. I was hoping to meet your Commanding Officer, Colonel Johnstone, but he is out on patrol, so I gather."

"Yes, sir. There have been reports of disturbances with Bannock people. They seem to have the jitters over the negotiations with the Mormons." He nodded to the waiting horses. "We are sending out another patrol soon – see if we can get any news from the Colonel. It isn't usual for him to be away from the Fort for so long."

"This used to be an old trading station, so I understand?"

"Yes sir. It burned down a couple of years ago, due to some dispute the Mormons had with old man Bridger over selling alcohol and the likes to—"

"All very interesting, Lieutenant, but I have no time for history lessons. I need a fresh horse and supplies for the ride. You set to it whilst I go and eat something from that grease spoon of a saloon you have here. I'll meet you back here in one hour."

Faulkner went to speak, but the man had gone, striding out of the livery stable with a steely determination, like someone possessed. Pushing his hat back on his head, Faulkner leaned back against a supporting post and let out a long sigh.

They rode out in silence, Faulkner long since giving up trying to engage the stern Federal agent in conversation. The man rode ramrod-straight in the saddle, seemingly impervious to the heat. Beside him, Faulkner consulted the map given to him by Porter, nothing more than a few lines sketched out with one or two compass points included to give some sense of direction. With no scale to guide him, it was difficult for Faulkner to work out how far away the site of the incident was, so he put as much of it out of his mind as he could, and rode along, eyes forever scanning the undulating landscape on all sides.

"You fought in the War, Lieutenant?"

The question came so unexpectedly, Faulkner started, voice catching in his throat. He swallowed hard. "War, sir? What war might that be?"

"The Mormon war, of course."

"Oh, no. No sir. I gained my commission last spring. This is my first posting."

A grunt and Cross grew silent again. Faulkner went to give further explanation, but decided against it, the man's rigid demeanour causing him to think that nothing he had to say would be of any interest to Cross at all.

They made camp amongst some thick scrub, tall rocks forming a natural sanctuary, allowing them some protection from a cruel cold wind, which took hold as soon as nighttime fell. Faulkner, wrapping himself in his blanket, huddled himself up into a tight ball.

"I'll take first watch."

Opening one eye, Faulkner stirred self-consciously, tiny needles of unease pricking at his neck. "Sir, I am sorry, I did not think we would need—"

"There's always a need, Lieutenant. As this is your first posting, you are not yet fully experienced in Frontier life. I am."

Faulkner considered the man again, his face lit by the fire he'd made with such casual ease. In the red glow, his features took on those of some fairy-tale goblin Faulkner took such pleasure in reading as a boy. Lying snuggled up in his bed, he'd turn each page with growing expectation of the next, devouring the words with relish, loving the thrill of the many stories to do with wicked witches, sprites, hobgoblins, dwarves and brave heroes. Like some of those characters, this man brought him a distinct sense of unease, but unlike them he was real and the safety of a blanket would not help in any altercation. Faulkner shivered and turned over, not wishing to gaze upon the man's sharp profile any more than he had to.

He awoke with a start, the sunlight beating down to strike his face, the smell of fresh coffee invading his nostrils. He sat up, rubbing his face.

"This'll wake you up," said Cross, handing over a tin cup full of steaming black coffee.

Taking it, Faulkner gazed up at the agent and frowned. "I thought we would share the watch."

Cross shrugged. "You were in such a deep sleep I thought it best to leave you."

"But, you shouldn't have, you should have—"

"Drink your coffee, Lieutenant, then do what you have to do. We leave as soon as possible." He put his hands in the small of his back and stretched, letting out a deep sigh. "I hate this Godforsaken place. Too much dust and never enough to eat." He patted his flat stomach. "We need to get this done. I get short-tempered if I don't eat."

Not so far from the Bear River, where the trail winds through large outcrops of jagged rocks, they found the remains of the stagecoach, the horse team and accoutrements long since stripped. Turned on its side, the shell of the stage body lay amongst the rock-strewn ground, broken open, the flaking painted woodwork bleached by the sun. Cross prodded the side panel with the toe of his boot, grunted, and wandered around, studying the baked earth. At one point, he got down on his haunches and picked up several spent cartridges. "Smith and Wesson," he drawled and stood up. "There's nothing here, Lieutenant."

Standing some way off with the horses, holding both sets of reins, Faulkner did his best to offer an encouraging smile. "Perhaps if we scout around some we might—"

"Perhaps. I heard back at the Fort some of the rivers around these parts are contaminated, so best not wander too close to them. The lack of rain has brought many animals down to die on the banks."

"Contaminated?" Faulkner shivered. "What the hell next?"

"Who knows. Locusts maybe."

"Huh? Locusts, what the hell are they?"

"Never mind. Biblical plagues is all. We could scout around here for the best part of the next ten years and find diddly." He pulled in a deep breath and squinted towards the western horizon. "I wonder what Porter thought we'd find here."

"The Major seemed to think it was important I brought you here. He didn't exactly say why."

"And you didn't think to ask him?"

"The Major does not take kindly to having his decisions questioned, sir."

Cross muttered something to himself and scuffed at the dirt with his boot. "How long have you known the Major for, Lieutenant?"

"Since I arrived at Bridger. A few months. Why?"

"He strikes you as being a stand-up sort of guy? Honest, diligent in his duties?"

Without thinking, Faulkner ran a finger under his collar. The sweat accumulated there, faster than only a moment or so ago. "I, er, couldn't really say, sir."

"Well, take a wild guess."

The man stood some twelve paces away, but his eyes glinted hard and unblinking, causing Faulkner to glance away, shifting his weight, the man's unerring gaze causing him discomfort. "Sir, I'm not quite sure what you mean."

"I'll tell you what I mean, Lieutenant. Is he a good officer? Yes or no?"

"I guess that depends on what you mean by 'good'."

"What is your interpretation of that word?"

"Fastidious, scrupulously fair, courageous, commanding respect."

Cross nodded. "Uh huh. And Porter bears all of those qualities?"

"How far will this go, sir?"

"Just between you and me." Cross sighed and stuck his thumbs in his waistband. "Just spit it out, for Christ's sake."

"Very well." Faulkner breathed deep and turned his face towards the Federal agent, matching his hard stare. "Major Porter is a shirker, a man of base habits who commands no respect amongst the men. It has long been the rumour that Colonel Johnstone is seeking to have him replaced because of his dallying with certain ladies."

"I see. And as to his honesty?"

A pause, during which Faulkner gnawed away at the inside of his cheek. "He has been known to take money. Bribes."

"A lot of money?"

"I couldn't say. It's not my place to—"

"Ease up, Lieutenant. What you've said so far is enough to reinforce my own opinions."

"You have suspicions he might—"

"Washington has long been uneasy about the killing of Senator Bowen. This was no random holdup, Lieutenant. Someone instigated the whole sorry affair to put the scuppers on any agreements made between Brigham Young and the President. Bowen's job was to smooth out any wrinkles in the negotiations. Someone wanted him to fail before he even began."

"And you think the Major knew of this?"

Cross screwed up his mouth. "I've been asking around. Over the past year, your good Major has made some dubious decisions. Last winter he put some Pinkerton detective in jail for an alleged killing. Seems this Pinkerton was innocent of all charges, but Porter tried his utmost to have him killed. Question is, why?"

"Because this detective had his own suspicions?" Cross nodded. "Then ... Dear God, then you believe Porter has made some sort of deal with the ones responsible for the Senator's death?"

"All I need do is prove it – get the evidence. There ain't none out here, that's for sure."

"So why send us?"

"To get us out the way, of course. He's up to something, and being here, seeing this place for what it is – a heap of crap in the desert sun – I am certain of it."

Nineteen

Behind his desk, Major Porter poured himself another good measure of whisky into a glass tumbler at his side and waved the partly-dressed woman out of his office.

"Same time tomorrow, Major?"

He peered at her over the rim of his glass, taking in the swell of her breasts and how they struggled to conceal themselves in the confines of her tightly-drawn bodice. He downed the drink, gasped and leered, "Honey, if I could spare the time, you'd be back here right now." He slapped his thigh. "Right here."

Placing a fingertip on her full lips, she bobbed around coyly, "Ah, Major, you are always ready to please."

He slowly got to his feet, cupping his crotch with one hand. "And you *do* please me, Maribel, you please me more than any other—"

The door flew open with a tremendous crash, causing both Porter and Maribel to jump and yelp. Porter glared at the out-of-breath sergeant filling the doorway. "What in the name of hell are you—"

"Beggin' your pardon, Major, but I think you had better come and see this."

Rumbling with indignation, Porter came around the desk, paused to plant a kiss on Maribel's cheek and said, "This had better be important, Sergeant."

"Oh, I think it is, sir. I think it is."

Pushing past the sergeant, Porter readjusted his tunic and stepped out into the glare of the sunshine, squinting as he did so. It took him a few moments for his eyes to readjust but when they did the sight before him caused his stomach to flip. He groaned, "Oh Jesus."

Across the churned up parade ground, Detective Simms dismounted from his horse, stretched his back and gestured for the man beside him to get down also. Porter recognised the man instantly and, in a low, conspiratorial tone, spoke through the side of his mouth to the Sergeant, "Get over there and find out what the merry hell they are doing here."

"It's one of them escaped prisoners, Major, the one you—"

"I know who the fuck it is, you dimwit. Go and find out why he's alive. You get me?"

"I, er, think so, sir."

"Delay 'em, give me time to send off a telegram."

The Sergeant gave a lazy salute and ambled across the dust-laden parade ground.

"Trouble, honey?"

Porter shot Maribel and sharp glance. "Nothing that can't be fixed. Get over to the saloon and find two of my boys in there – Corporals Baxter and Coulson. You'll see them by the stripes on their arms."

"I think I know who they are. They rode in yesterday afternoon, telling everyone how their companions had gotten themselves lost out in the prairie."

"Yes," Porter ran the back of his hand across his brow, "that's them. I sent out four of 'em, and only two came back. But they will be well recovered by now, so set to it, Maribel – time is not on our side!"

Simms sighed when he saw the big lumbering figure of a sergeant waddling towards him. Over on the far side, he noticed a smaller man scurrying across towards the telegraph office. Her nudged Brewster beside him. "Is that the officer you mentioned?"

"That's him all right."

Simms turned to Deep Water. "Position yourself on the far side, under the shadow of that ramshackle collection of buildings yonder. Take my Root rifle with you."

"You expect there to be shooting?" The Indian looked nervous, his eyes darting around the confines of the Fort. All around people were loading up wagons, standing chatting idly in groups, horses moving this way and that, with soldiers in the lookout tower. Nobody seemed particularly tense until Deep Water followed Simms's gaze and eyed the officer disappearing into the telegraph office. He grunted. "Ah. I understand." Simms threw him the rifle and the scout checked it and slipped out of sight.

Simms moved the Colt Navy in its holster and nodded to Brewster. "If there's shooting, you keep down."

"And cheat the hang man, is that what you mean?"

"No, I mean I'm going to put in a good word. I told you. If you end up getting yourself shot, none of it will mean very much, will it?"

"I guess not."

"I need to see some identification."

Simms turned to see the owner of the voice – the big, burly sergeant now standing before him, one hand resting on his own revolver, the other thrust out, palm upturned.

"I can show you that," said Simms and drew back his coat to reveal his sheriff's star pinned to his shirt. The sergeant could get a good look at the Smith and Wesson Model One in its shoulder holster too. "I'm sheriff over at Bovey. Send a telegram to check, just like your boss has just done over there."

Frowning, the sergeant turned.

Emerging from a small building, Major Porter strode determinedly towards them, his face set hard, mouth a thin line, eyes blazing with barely-contained anger.

"Ah shit," breathed the sergeant and took a step backwards.

"Simms!"

Porter stepped up close, hand extended. Simms looked at it. "Major."

Porter's arm dropped, somewhat self-consciously. He flashed a humourless grin from Simms to the sergeant. "Dismissed, Sergeant Agnew."

Hesitating, the sergeant's face crumpled up. Simms, studying the man, thought he was in pain.

"I believed you wanted me to—"

"*Dismissed*," snapped Porter, that maniacal grin of his frozen into his features. "Miss Maribel will meet with you in the saloon."

It took a moment or two for Agnew to disentangle any hidden meaning in Porter's words before the sergeant took off his hat, ran a hand through his hair and blew out his cheeks. "Yes, sir. Whatever you say, sir." And, readjusting his hat, he moved away.

The tension crackled in the air. Simms, feet slightly apart, allowed his hand to swing close to the Navy Colt.

"Surprised to see you here, Simms," said Porter, following Agnew's retreating back, "wasn't sure if I'd ever see you again."

"And why might that be?"

"Oh, you know … " He looked at the detective. "Things happen. Accidents. Sickness. Matrimonial strife. How is that miserable squaw of yours? Still making your pecker sing and dance?"

Without a pause, Simms swung a punch, a hard left cross, which snapped the Major's head to the side as if hit by a sledgehammer. Legs giving way under him, he dropped to his knees, dazed.

Behind him, Brewster squawked and Simms turned, low, swivelling from the hip, the Navy coming up in a blur, one fluid, uninterrupted movement, easing back the hammer and pointing the revolver directly towards Agnew who, reacting to the suddenness of the incident, returned and stepped up closer, reaching for his own gun.

"Drop that nice and easy, sergeant."

Agnew's gun was not halfway clear of its holster. For one agonising moment, it seemed he might continue to draw, but better judgement prevailed and, holding up his free hand, he gently took out the gun and let it fall to the ground.

"Pick it up, Brewster."

"What?"

"Pick the goddamned gun *up*."

Brewster floundered, lips trembling, eyes locked on Agnew. He took a step.

Next to them, Porter groaned.

Simms kept his gun on the sergeant, who quivered from head to foot, sweat patches under his serge blue uniform growing noticeably. As Brewster bent down to pick up the sergeant's gun, Porter made a gurgling noise. "Bastard," he muttered.

From out of the saloon came two men, marching forward with the look of stone-cold killers written across their faces. Young and mean looking, both of them held pistols, the one on the left holding a hand-gun so big it looked more like a miniature canon.

"Brewster, you stay on your knees. That boy there is toting a Colt Walker, the biggest goddamned gun you've ever seen. It hits you – anywhere – and you are dead. Sergeant, hightail out of here." Simms made a deep frown towards Agnew who continued to quiver deep down into his boots. "*Scoot*, you mangy cur!"

Agnew needed no further encouragement and waddled off in the closest he could get to a run.

From ten or so paces away, the two soldiers stopped. "You're a dead man, cowboy," spat the lanky soldier with the Walker in his fist. He dropped to his knees and put the barrel of the big gun across his left forearm, which acted like a sort of rest, and eased back the hammer.

The first shot hit him between the eyes, a perfect black hole, about the size of a dime. A look of startled amazement flickered across his eyes before he crumpled to his side into the ground, a pool of blood and brain blossoming around the back of what remained of his head.

Things accelerated from that point.

Simms knew things were going wrong when the soldier with the Walker dropped. He looked down at his own gun, wondering if he had inadvertently set off a shot. Of course, he knew he hadn't, but he needed to check anyway. The shot was a damned good one, Deep Water's ability with firearms always impressive. Acting swiftly, Simms glanced across towards the line of outbuildings set against the far wall of the Fort. People were flying around in every direction, the gunfire causing them to stampede, but of the Indian scout he could see no sign.

Out of the corner of his eye, he spotted Porter sitting up. Before Simms could stop it, the Major put a round into Brewster's back. Without a thought for his own safety, Simms went to his stricken charge, mindless of the second soldier bearing down on him. When another shot took this soldier in the throat, Simms realised nothing was going to go right with this day.

"Bastard," said Porter in a shaky voice, and Simms glanced backwards to see him climbing unsteadily to his feet. His service revolver was in his hand, but he appeared disorientated, still groggy from the blow Simms landed on his temple. "Bastard."

Quickly checking Brewster still lived, Simms ran up to Porter, tore the revolver from the Major's grip and was about to club him with it when he caught a movement to his right. He turned to look and Porter took his chance, running like a drunkard towards the telegraph, pushing frightened bystanders out of his way in his mad rush.

Breathing hard, Simms settled his gaze upon two men riding through the main entrance. Soldiers gathered around, appearing from their various sentry posts, guns readied, nervous, uncertain. They waited whilst one of the riders, a young and eager-looking lieutenant, edged his horse closer. Next to him rode a hawkish individual with hard features and piercing blue eyes.

"You'll be Simms," said the hawk. "My named is Cross, and I am a Federal agent, sent across from Washington to investigate the killing of a certain Senator Bowen. Perhaps you have heard of him?"

Simms said nothing, all of his attention centred on the young officer as he dismounted. Assessing the situation, he drew his revolver.

"Before we get any further into this," said the officer, "you are under arrest."

Simms sighed but didn't argue, raising both his arms as the soldiers closed in.

Twenty

Morris spoke through his teeth, trying his utmost not to appear nervous despite his insides rolling around like a small boat tossed in a hurricane. "Jasper, you just keep nice and still. You have that carbine close at hand."

"I do," said Jasper, using one hand to lean upon the sideboard whilst his other held the barrel of the carbine.

"Any sign of trouble, you shoot the big fella in the middle, the one with the red coat. I reckon he's the leader."

"They look mean," whispered Millie as she poked her head from out of the wagon interior.

"Hush now," said her mother, "go back inside and don't make a sound."

Morris chewed noisily on a plug of tobacco. "Your youngens inside your wagon, Jasper?"

"Uh huh. Constance has my Colt with her. She'll die before she lets these heathens get anywhere near her or the children."

"Let us pray it doesn't come to that."

"Amen."

He held up his hand in the universal sign of greeting as the small band of warriors drew nearer. "Howdy there, folks." He wasn't at all sure if these were appropriate words to use to such people, and the word felt awkward in his mouth, but anything was better than silence.

They stopped some ten or so paces away, their ponies whickering and snorting, each man's face nut brown and deeply lined, eyes wide an unblinking as they all studied the travellers with acute interest. Each warrior was dressed differently, three of them bare-chested, their bodies lean and superbly muscled. One wore no leggings, his thighs rippling where he gripped his pony. Two wore buckskin shirts, or vests, whilst the one in the centre donned a military-style scarlet coloured tunic, unbuttoned, revealing a breast protector fashioned from two strung-together rows of hollowed out bones. A single feather adorned his head.

Each man held either a lance, or a heavy-headed club, with bows over their shoulders, knives at the hips. None carried a firearm.

For a long while, nobody spoke. Arabella grew irritated, her hand brushing her husband's thigh. "What do you think they want?"

"Ain't sure," said Morris, the smile set in his face like a permanent feature. "If they meant to kill us, I reckon they'd have done so by now." He lifted his voice, "We're passin' through is all. Heading for Salt Lake."

This seemed to cause no change upon the small group, who sat astride their mounts as impassive as when they had first appeared. Somewhere in the distance a buzzard screeched. Arabella squeezed his arm. "Ask them again what they want."

"They don't understand," whispered Morris. Slowly he moved his hand from left to right in a broad sweep. "We is just travellers. We mean no harm."

The silence continued, each Indian face unreadable. Morris pulled in a breath and was about to speak when the red-coated one shifted, turned and muttered something to the warrior next to him. A slight kick against his pony's flank and he moved forward, eyes scanning the two wagons, assessing everything he saw.

"We trade."

It took a moment for Morris to react. He looked askance at Jasper, then to his wife, then shrugged and grinned towards the speaker. "Trade? What might you be trading, friend?"

Remaining expressionless, the warrior turned and barked something at his companions. Two detached themselves from the others, dismounting with the grace of young deer, light-footed, barely making a sound. They untied the bulging cloth bags slung over the croup of their mounts and delved inside.

Morris watched in stunned silence as the warriors brought out hunks of meat, still dripping with blood. Deer, perhaps buffalo, he didn't care. If the others felt like he did, they would already be imagining roasting the flesh over a campfire, filling their bellies for the first time in days.

"Dear Lordy," he managed.

"Don't cuss," snapped Arabella. She leaned across her husband and looked the Indian directly in the eyes. "What would you be wanting?"

"In exchange," put in Jasper quickly, careful not to make any movement towards his gun.

The slightest frown creased the warrior's face, and he gestured for the others to move forward with the meat, which they did. Jasper took the great hunks from their arms. "Thank you," he said, and bowed.

From the second wagon, Constance, Jasper's only daughter, appeared, her bare feet scuffing up little billows of dust as she drew closer. In her little arms she carried a pile of blankets. Thick, warm, woollen blankets.

"Oh my," said Jasper, spotting her.

The other warriors grew animated, several laughing. Redcoat jumped down from his pony and skipped forward, eyes and mouth wide. With great reverence, he took the blankets, turned his eyes towards Jasper and gave a deep bow of gratitude.

"Looks like we have a trade," said Arabella, unable to keep the relief from her voice.

Later that evening, they sat around a campfire, all of them partaking of the meat the Indians had brought. They sat huddled in their new blankets and although nobody could understand what either was saying, the atmosphere was relaxed and genial. Some hours later, when the warriors finally did leave, it was smiles and waves all around.

"They ain't savages at all," commented Arabella, standing beside her husband, arms folded, smiling, watching the band moving silently away.

"Well, not them at least."

"Wonder what kind they was," said Jason. "The man at the mercantile store said Utes is worse, but then another customer said they was *all* just a bunch of godless savages."

"Well, seems they were all wrong," said Arabella, and ruffled her son's head. "This land is full of surprises."

And the next day, when they set off in the early morning, they were in for another surprise.

Amongst a narrow gully, they found the body of a man. Jason and Castor, running ahead, found him first and flagged down the following wagons. Morris and Jasper eased the horses to a halt in the confines of that small pass and immediately ran over to the man whilst Arabella soaked a cloth in water.

"He's alive," gasped Castor.

"He won't be for much longer if we don't get some water into him," said Arabella, and gestured for the two men to pick up the body. "Get him inside Jasper's wagon."

It took them a lot of grunting and groaning, but eventually they managed to heave the poor man into the wagon. Arabella moved up beside him, mopped his brow and dabbed water on his swollen, cracked lips and when at last there came a tiny rattle from deep within his throat, she gave a little holler of triumph.

He was going to live.

Twenty-One

"I'm here to speak with Major Porter," said the hawkish man called Cross through the bars of the cell in which Simms sat, running the brim of his hat through his fingers. "He sent us on a wholly unwarranted journey across the range and I need to hear his explanation."

"I have some serious questions I'd like to put to him also," said Simms without looking up. "If you let me out of this damned cell, I could perhaps ask him."

Through the main door came the young officer, two soldiers closely behind. The Lieutenant pulled off his hat and placed it on the nearby desk. He appeared hot, lines of worry written hard across his face. "He's nowhere to be found," he said.

"That's just dandy," breathed Simms.

"What in the hell do you mean," said the hawk, turning on the Lieutenant, his face reddening with anger. "He couldn't have gotten far, for God's sake. Have you searched every square foot of this rat-infested shithole?"

The Lieutenant bristled for a moment before releasing a long stream of air. "Mr. Cross, my men have looked everywhere and he has gone. If you want to conduct your own search, then feel free to do so. But his horse has gone."

"And whoever shot those two troopers? No doubt he has absconded too."

The Lieutenant shrugged and went to the desk from where he picked up Simms's Navy Colt. "They weren't killed with this, or this," he pointed to the Smith and Wesson. "So, we have a conundrum."

"That being the case," said Simms, standing up, "perhaps you could let me out."

"Not just yet." The Lieutenant moved over to the cell. "Who was the man you were with, the one wounded by the Major?"

"His name is Brewster, an escaped convict. My orders were to bring him in, which I have done. Porter then decided to shoot him."

"Why would he do that?" asked Cross.

"Exactly the question I wanted to ask the good Major myself." Simms gripped the bars. "Lieutenant, the longer we debate all this, the longer it's gonna take to bring that sonofabitch back here. He's up to something, has been since the day I first laid eyes on him."

"Well," said the Lieutenant, "a girl over in the saloon, one of the Major's playthings, she seems to confirm some of what you're saying. According to her, Porter had those two dead troopers in his pay. Derelicts they were. Apparently, the Major sent them together with two others out into the Territory. They came back with their tails between their legs."

"Four? That means two of 'em are still—"

"The other two are missing, presumed dead."

Cross cleared his throat, "I have nothing to prove this but I suspect those men were sent out to waylay the good Lieutenant and myself."

The Lieutenant gawped. "What? You never mentioned that before."

Cross gave an easy smile, "I tend to think things through before I spout them off, Lieutenant Faulkner."

Faulkner screwed up the corner of his mouth and didn't appear convinced. "I reckon that's a theory too far, Mr. Cross. But we have the Sergeant confined to barracks and I shall question him directly."

Simms interjected, "And Brewster?"

"He's in the infirmary. Medical officer says he'll get through."

"Good. With his testimony, together with the sergeant's, we'll have enough evidence to put Porter away until we found out what the merry hell is going on."

"That is my remit, Detective," said Cross. "I was sent here to investigate the assassination of Senator Bowen. Like I say, I've found nothing so far to implicate Porter, but his behaviour has been erratic and deeply suspicious to say the least."

"He was coming out of the telegraph office," said Simms. "First thing you could do is find out what message he sent, and to whom."

Cross nodded. "I will. Lieutenant, get this man out of this cell. We need him."

Simms came out of the infirmary, chewing his lip. The Lieutenant was standing beside the small parade ground, deep in conversation with Cross. Two or three prairie schooners trundled by, the bonnets bulging, pots and pans clanging against the sides, excited children screaming and shouting. Simms watched them with mild interest, silently wishing them good fortune.

"I'm still troubled by the death of those troopers," said the Lieutenant, moving up to the detective. "I am convinced you had an accomplice."

"Well, I haven't."

"I've been making enquiries, Simms. Seems you were incarcerated on a previous occasion here in Bridger, and an accomplice broke you out."

"That was different. Your good Major Porter was looking to have me dangling from a rope for something I didn't do."

"It all seems mighty fishy to me. Those two having the drop on you and them ending up dead, shot from a distance."

"Puts me in the clear then, don't it."

"Maybe. Maybe not. " He glanced towards Cross. "What's your take on this?"

"My *take* is that Porter is up to something and is in *so* deep he has only one thought on his mind – survival. I want Detective Simms to lead me across the prairie and find Porter. Only then, when he is apprehended, can we get to the bottom of all of this."

The Lieutenant looked towards Simms. "I'm not comfortable with any of this. Major Porter is a commissioned officer in the United States Army. That says a lot. I am deeply troubled by the notion of him having dealings with cutthroats and the like."

Simms gave a half smile. "If it's any consolation," said the Pinkerton, "he hoodwinked me too. I suspected there was something, but I never knew what."

Faulkner bristled, his jaw line growing red. "He never *hoodwinked* me, Mr. Simms. *If* he has lied, then he has disgraced the uniform he wears. For that, he will pay."

It took them less than half a day to find them. Riding over a slight rise, Simms reined in his horse and leaned forward in his saddle, peering down into the base of the little gully. Surrounded by cliffs and sagebrush, the clearing was an almost perfect circle of bare, barren soil. In its centre, Porter sat on his knees, stripped naked, hands bound behind his back.

"What in the name of hell happened to him?"

Simms looked across at Cross and shrugged. "Let's ask him, shall we."

Throughout the journey back to Fort Bridger, they got little sense from the Major. Traumatised by whatever had happened to him, he trembled and moaned but uttered no meaningful words. Simms fashioned a cloak for him out of his bedroll so that when they came through the main gates, despite the many stares and bemused expressions, the Major retained some hint of dignity.

In his old office, they sat him down in the corner, Cross giving him water, helping him by holding his head still and tipping an old enamel cup to his dried lips.

From the doorway, the young lieutenant looked on. Simms came in. He had gone to the barracks and found several items of clothing. These he passed over to Cross who, giving him a hard stare, nevertheless helped the distraught and still shocked Major into a shirt and uniform trousers.

"He was like this when you found him?"

Simms nodded towards Faulkner. "Just sitting there, almost as if he was waiting."

"But why?"

"I guess because somebody placed him there."

"Might just as well have put a signpost pointing in his direction," said Cross, stepping away, studying Porter more closely. "He's scared to death."

"I saw things like this during the War," said Simms matter-of-factly. "Usually after some battle, or an ambush. Just knocks all the sense out of a man."

"You were in the War," said Cross, eyeing Simms with renewed interest. "Mexican War?"

"The very same."

"I served too."

Something passed between them, a sort of grudging respect, and Simms regarded Cross keenly, the same way Cross looked at him.

"Still doesn't tell us what happened to him," said Faulkner. "But I got a copy of the telegrams he sent."

The others turned to him. "And?" said Simms.

"It seems he has a contact in Kansas City. A man by the name of Moss. Porter sent two messages, warning him that you, Mr. Simms, were close to 'putting everything at risk'. Those were his exact words."

Chewing his lip, Simms instinctively drew his Navy and checked the cylinder. "Moss. A lot of this is beginning to make sense to me now."

"Care to share any of this?" said Cross.

"It's something I never thought of before, not until now," said the detective. "I received a telegram of my own, ordering me to bring in three escaped convicts, awaiting sentence for the robbing of a stage." He turned to Lieutenant Faulkner. "The one in which Senator Bowen was murdered."

"It was an assassination," interjected Cross.

"Exactly. Those men were a threat to whoever planned the whole damned thing. They had to be silenced, one way or another."

"So they got you to bring them in, with the hope that what, you'd kill them?"

"Maybe. Or maybe we'd all be killed out there, in the Territory. No questions asked. We'd simply disappear."

"Those two troopers," said the lieutenant, "Barker and Coulson. They'd rode out some weeks ago, with two others. They were under Porter's orders, but I didn't question it, believing them to be going on a routine scouting party."

"But now you think differently?"

Faulkner nodded at Simms. "It fits. All of it fits. Four of them went out, only two came back. And now those two are dead. Maybe the person who shot them is also in on this."

"I doubt it."

"Why do you said that so emphatically?" said Cross.

"Because the same person who put those two ingrates down is the same person who trussed up Porter for us to find so easily." He smiled. "Don't ask me how I know, I just do. I'm going to find out where that telegram I received originated from. In the meantime, see if you can get any sense out of him." He pointed at Porter. "I'll then be riding over to Laramie and pick up a stage to Kansas City. Me and Mr. Moss have some serious talking to be doing."

Twenty-Two

"My name is Dixon. I'm a US Marshal , on my way to Twin Buttes when I was set upon by Indians."

"Oh my," said the attractive, fresh-faced young woman sitting beside him. Turning towards the open end of the wagon where a large man, presumably her husband, and three children were all stood, staring wide-eyed at the recovering stranger, she said, "He says Indians did this to him."

"Can't be the same ones we came across, Arabella," said the man quickly. He stared directly towards Dixon. "They ain't all bad."

"No," said Dixon, "but some are."

"Name's Richard Morris," said the man. "These are my children – Millie, Jason and Castor. We left Fort Bridger over a week ago now, heading across to Salt Lake City where we plan to meet up with our brethren. We're Mormons. Thought you'd best know that, seeing as some people find us somewhat strange."

"Well, not me." Propped up by a heap of thick pillows, Dixon sighed and closed his eyes, more comfortable than he had felt for months. If this was good, old-fashioned hospitality then he wanted more of it. His eyes flickered open. "I want to thank you for everything you've done, ma'am." He smiled at Arabella, sat beside him. In the confines of the wagon she was so close he could smell her perfume. Strange, he thought, for her to be wearing perfume whilst out on the range.

She ran the back of her fingers across his brow. They were cool and soft and he sank back into the pillows, luxuriating on how such good fortune could visit him after suffering so many deprivations. He pondered on his many blessings, thinking he should take up religion, give thanks.

"We all thought you was gonna die."

He caught the concern in her voice, the softness of her green eyes. "It's all down to you, ma'am. Without your care, I doubt I would have made it. How did you find me?"

"Sheer chance," said Morris. "You say Indians set upon you?"

"A bunch of naked savages they were," said Dixon. "I killed a couple, but then one of them got me in the shoulder. The pain of it is the last thing I remember."

Arabella's finger slowly slipped from his brow. "We think you must have fallen from the nearby rocks."

"Yeah, maybe so."

"You were lucky you fell the way you did – your landing pushed the arrow almost all the way out. But you have a lot more wounds. Bullet wounds."

"Yes. I was bushwhacked by some loathsome types, tended by a friend and then, as I was getting myself back on my feet, the Indians attacked."

"Seems like you've had a lot of scrapes, feller."

He smiled towards Morris, standing there so big across the shoulders. A tough, grizzled face, panhandles for hands gripping the edge of the tailgate. As humourless as his wife was kind and open. "It's my line of work. Not many of us get to make it past fifty."

"And how old might you be?" asked one of the boys.

"*Castor,*" snapped Arabella, "you know better than to be so impertinent."

"It's quite all right," said Dixon and he smiled towards the boy. "I'm fifty-three."

For the next three days, they made steady progress, never deviating from the trail. They met up with a group of other travellers, who greeted them with cheery smiles. They shared food, the children fetching water from the nearby river. That night, they camped amongst the trees, the oxen wandering off, causing mischief with a dog belonging to one of the other families.

"Them cattle seem awful thin," observed one old man, sitting with his back against a wagon wheel, drinking from a stone jug. He spoke with a curious accent.

Dixon, still uncertain on his feet, sniffed loudly and collapsed next to him. "Smells like whisky."

"It is," said the old man with a chuckle and handed it over. "You ain't a Mormon, then?"

Taking a large swallow, Dixon put his head back, closed his eyes and allowed the liquid to percolate down into the depths of his being. "No sir, I ain't." He took another swallow and handed the jug back. He noted the revolver stuck in the man's waistband and pursed his lips. "I do believe that is a Dean and Adams revolver you have there, mister."

The man's mouth formed an 'O' and tapped the gun handle with a finger. "It is that. Double-action, issued to myself back when I served in the British Army."

"Ah, so you're British."

"I am. From Lancashire, England. My family and I made the journey across the Atlantic some six or so months ago, hearing it was 'the land of opportunity'. Pah," he turned away and spat into the ground before taking another slug. "Not two weeks into the trail I lost my wife and son from cholera. That's what I thought when I saw your cattle. Ours went the same way. This land is brutal and unforgiving but you look as though you already know that."

Dixon smiled and accepted the jug once more. He took a drink. "Yes I do." He shifted uneasily, his backside already uncomfortable on the hard, compacted earth beneath him. "I was ambushed by Indians and those good people," he pointed across to where Morris and the others were gathered around the campfire, "they took me in."

"And you've joined them? You've converted?"

"Converted? Hell no, I ain't religious – not for any kind of religion. I've seen too damn much to believe in a caring, forgiving God."

"Isn't that the point, though? God is not here to interfere, merely to guide and help when we reach out."

"And your kin dying of cholera, that was His way of helping you?"

A wry smile. He lifted the whisky jug and drank. "He led me to the bottle, my friend. It is all I have now."

"You take it well."

"I've had a lot of practise." He chuckled again, put his hand around the wheel rim and hauled himself to his feet. "But even I have to surrender to nature. I need my bed." He offered the jug again, and again Dixon took it and swallowed it down. "Keep it until the morning. I'll sleep like a babe so I won't be needing any more this night."

He waddled off and Dixon watched him clambering into the back of one of the wagons tied down amongst the trees. Lifting the jug, he studied it for a long while before taking yet another mouthful.

In the morning, Dixon woke to a great commotion. Sitting up, he blinked through the last remaining vestiges of sleep, rubbed his eyes and saw the gathering of people outside the same wagon the old man went to sleep in.

"What's happened," he called out to Jasper, who went stumbling by.

"He's dead," said Jasper and continued across to the group.

Dixon smacked his lips, eyed the empty jug beside him, rolled over and tried to get some more sleep.

"It's the weirdest thing," Morris was saying as he hitched up the team to his wagon. Dixon sat on the driver's seat, playing absently with the loose reins. "They found him like that, eyes wide open, dead as a post. Who'd have believed it?"

"Did anyone say how he died?"

"No. Some are saying cholera, like his kin, but there we no signs." He stepped away to admire his handiwork and patted the nearest horse on the rump. "Maybe it was just old age. The guy was all petered out."

"Seemed mighty sprightly to me."

"He did, huh? Well, just shows you, you never can tell." He wiped his face with his neckerchief and looked up to the sky, blowing out a loud sigh. "Damn, it is getting hot. Some of the other folk said we need to follow the trail even more closely towards Salt Lake, as Indians are desperate for food and water. A pity you don't have a gun. You being a Marshal, I reckon you could be fairly good."

"I am." He shrugged. "Maybe we could buy one from some of the other folk?"

"They're heading north, so it is my reckoning they'll need all the firearms they have."

"North? To Twin Buttes?" He swivelled in the seat, "That was my destination. Perhaps I could ride along with them?"

"Well, you could, yes of course. We'd be awfully sorry to see you go though."

Dixon grinned. "In that case, I'll just tag along with you."

Morris smiled, gave the horse a hearty slap and went over to Jasper, who was struggling to put his own team together.

The heat pounded down upon them, making their journey slow and arduous, forcing them to stop and rest often. At a place Morris told them was Bear River, they went down to take water, whilst Arabella remained behind with Dixon.

"He's a good man, your husband."

"Yes he is." She turned to him. "Are you?"

"Depends what you mean by good." He smiled. "I'm a lawman, Arabella. That means I sometimes have to do what is necessary."

"Killing, you mean?"

He nodded. "Unfortunately. It does not please me when I say I have put more than one man in the ground – but none that did not deserve it."

"I'm not sure if *any* man deserves it, Mr. Dixon. The Lords teaches us it is a sin to kill."

"Yes. And yet you slaughter wild beasts to eat. Is that not killing?"

"Hardly the same."

"Really? Does the good Lord make a distinction?"

She took a deep breath. "You speak as if you have some knowledge of the Good Book, Mr. Dixon."

Pulling in a breath, Dixon closed his eyes for a moment before saying, " '*Every moving thing that lives shall be food for you.*' I believe that is a quote from Genesis, chapter nine."

"I am impressed."

"My mother was a Sunday school teacher. She knew the Bible as well as anyone I have ever known – better than most. She read it daily, to me and my brothers, back when we was young. She was a fine woman, my mother. She is still alive."

"My. She must be aged?"

"Eighty-seven years old," he said with a smile. "Constitution of an ox, although looking at your scraggy specimens that doesn't say much."

"Richard is of a mind to slaughter them. It was not our intention. We had hoped to put them in a small holding when we reached Salt Lake. "

"Plans have a way of unravelling."

He looked at her and she held his gaze. "Indeed they do."

The following day they encountered a group of four Indians down by the river. They were emaciated and one of them lay on the ground, the others looking on helpless.

"We have to help them," said Arabella.

Morris, whose pallor was not as healthy looking as it had been, dragged a shaking hand across his brow. "I'm not sure if that is such a good idea."

"You cover me with your carbine," said Dixon, "I'll go parlay with 'em."

"Are you sure that is wise? What if they turn nasty?"

"Then you shoot 'em." Dixon winked and climbed down. He stretched out his limbs and rubbed his inner thigh, where the old wound continued to throb. Holding out his hands to show he was un-armed, he approached the group with slow, deliberate steps.

Standing motionless, the Indians observed him. They had hatchets and knives in the waistbands, and two held bows, both of which were ready.

"You Kiowa? I speak some Kiowa?"

Their blank expression gave him his reply and he sighed and, with his right hand held up, he stepped over to the stricken brave on the ground. He looked the colour of death and there were black slug trails running from his nose and mouth.

"Shit. Looks like he is poisoned." He pointed towards the water. "You drink from there?" Another blank look, so he mimed raising a water canteen to his mouth and drinking from it. The Indians muttered amongst themselves, then barked something to him which he took to be the affirmative. He shrugged, looked at the Indian on the ground again, and dragged a forefinger across his throat. "*Muerte*," he said in Spanish. This single word caused them to grow agitated and they gaggled amongst themselves. He took three paces back, arms outstretched, shouting back towards the wagon, "Get that goddamned gun ready."

But Arabella's voice came back, confused, worried, "Mr. Dixon, he ain't right."

Dixon turned and saw it was so. Morris appeared bent over, clutching at his guts, retching. "Shit." The Marshal swung around to face the Indians, who were stressed, faces black with anger, and he pulled out the Adams revolver from the back of his waistband and blasted all three of with well placed shots, the doubler-action revolver allowing the discharge to be fast and effective.

With Arabella's screams ringing in his ears, he stepped amongst the fallen braves. Two were dead, the third writhing at his feet. He put a shot through the man's head, then went across and did the same to one already dying.

He helped himself to the best of the knives and hatchets, then strode back to the wagon. Millie was coming out of the wagon, her eyes red-rimmed, lips trembling. "Why you shoot 'em?"

Before he could answer, Jasper emerged from the other wagon, his Colt Navy in his hand, hammer cocked. "And where in the hell did you get that gun, mister?"

It was then Dixon realised he had a lot of explaining to do.

Twenty-Three

"I may as well come clean with you, Mr. Simms," said Brewster, lying in a narrow bed, the sweat-stained sheets stinking almost as much as him.

"Anything you can tell me will aid you, Brewster. I ain't making no promises, but—"

"I can," said Cross, standing close by. "I can and I will." He bent down and studied Brewster with his piercing blue eyes. "I am a Federal agent, son, here to investigate the death of Senator Bowen. You tell us what in the hell has been going on and I can guarantee your sentence will be commuted. If it leads to the arrest of the perpetrators, I can even go so far as to say you will serve no more than fifteen years. Maybe even ten."

"Holy Moses, you would do that for me, Mr. Federal agent, sir?"

"Yes, I will."

"So," said Simms, "there you have it Brewster. You've told us a lot so far, but do you know anything of Major Porter's involvement?"

"No. Not a thing. That was all Curly's doing. He didn't include us in his conversations with that bastard, but I'll tell you this. There is someone who might know. And I'll tell you for why too."

Simms and Cross exchanged a look. "Then tell it."

"Ben Magee, sheriff over at Fairweather, just a ways up from Needle Rocks. The plan was for us to meet up there after we held up the stage and divide up the money. Well, when we got there, Magee hauls us into his jail and that's when the Army came and took us away. It was Magee who dobbed us in. When we broke out of prison, Curly said he was gonna kill that bastard, just as soon as he spoke with Silas over at Twin Buttes. Poor old Curly never made it that far, as you know. And that is all there is. All of it."

"Why didn't you mention this Magee before," said Simms.

"I didn't trust you. I didn't think you would deliver me any sort of pardon, but now …" He nodded towards Cross, "Now I see that we could have a deal."

Cross expelled air nosily through his nostrils. "If this Magee is a part of this whole sorry mess and can lead us to the brains behind it all, you will be rewarded Mr. Brewster – I promise you that."

"He knows something, all right. Curly always suspected there was someone pulling all the strings, but he said he never asked too many questions, thinking it might be dangerous. Seems he was right."

"You have heard of this Silas from Twin Buttes?"

Simms grinned at Cross. "Oh yeah, I know him all right."

"Then we have some investigating to do. We shall set out at first light. I shall inform Lieutenant Faulkner and instruct him to keep the Major under lock and key until we return." He turned to Brewster and doffed his hat. "I'm obliged, son. The Government is anxious to have this whole business sorted out as quickly as possible so we can conclude our negotiations with those Latter Day Saints over in Salt Lake. If you have aided us in that, you won't be feeling that noose around your neck."

They went outside and Cross, putting both hands on his hips, stretched out his back and took in the air. "Damned hot."

"It'll be hotter out on the range. Not unlike how it was in the War."

"Long time ago, friend."

"Yep, but you never lose it. At least, that's my experience."

"Most of my time since I left the Army I have spent behind a desk in Washington. I have a house, with a backyard. Under the shade of a laburnum tree, my wife sits on a white painted bench and reads her books. I come home, we eat our dinner, and we got to bed. This is the first time I've been in the saddle for getting on ten years, Detective. I am in your debt for whatever help and guidance you can give."

"You don't look as if you've lost your edge."

"I will be honest with you – I have been in gunfights. Two, to be accurate. I practise every day, keep my eye in, so to speak. But you, I suspect, have a far greater experience of this Frontier life."

"Since being posted here, I don't think a month has gone by without me having to pull my gun from its holster. It is a dangerous land, Cross. I'm not sure people back east know just how dangerous." He shook his head, allowing his eyes to travel across the parade ground to where more pilgrims prepared wagons for their journey. "And it is my opinion it is going to get worse."

"What makes you say that?"

"Rumours. Scraps of news here and there. There's rumblings of people wanting to secede."

"Nothing will come of it."

"What if something does?"

"The Government will sort it all, Detective Simms. Why, are you concerned your position out here in the Territory might be compromised?"

"Hardly. I am in the somewhat enviable position of having duel responsibilities – I am a Pinkerton *and* a town sheriff. No, my concern is more for the ordinary people. Many are barely able to scratch a living out here. Anything which might threaten their often precarious situations would not be welcome – at least, not in my mind."

"I take it you too have managed to eke out some sort of life for yourself out here."

"I have, but it has not been easy. I lost my woman and my child but have since found a kind of happiness. I have a small ranch, a few horses, some land for grazing. It's not much, but we get by."

"We? So, you have found someone else?"

"It happens."

"Yes, yes it does. My wife and I, we have no children. She cannot."

"Well, then I envy you, Mr. Cross – there is no greater pain than the loss of a child. Even one that had not already taken its first breath. She died giving birth. Such is the way of things."

"Yes. The world moves on and now we have a job to do. You are an extraordinary man, Mr. Simms. I am proud to be riding alongside you."

"Well, we ain't set for riding yet." He chuckled and readjusted his gun belt. "First light, you say?"

"Indeed, yes."

"Then I'll gather up our supplies." He stepped down and crossed the parade ground, feeling Cross's eyes boring into his back. A man who spent his life behind a desk might be something of a handicap, but even so, there was something dangerous about Cross that caused Simms to convince himself he needed to be on his guard. Night and day.

Twenty-Four

Things happened quickly over the course of the next few days.

Jasper, keeping his gun trained on Dixon, insisted the others tied the Marshal up.

"There has to be another way," said Arabella.

But Jasper wasn't having any of it. He instructed his son Rupert how to tie the knots, as both the older Morris boys, crunched up in tight balls beside their father's wagon, writhed in their own vomit and diarrhoea. When he'd finished Rupert stepped away, looked towards his friends, face ashen. "What is happening?"

Whilst Arabella rushed backwards and forwards with damp rags soaked in boiling water from an iron pot sitting upon the campfire, Dixon sat against Jasper's front wheel and watched. "I seen this before," he said through clenched teeth.

"You shut up," said Jasper, the gun shaking in his fist.

"You take it easy with that there revolver," said Dixon as one of the children ran up to her father.

Jasper snapped his head to face his daughter. "What is it?"

"Pa," said Constance, breathless, wringing her hands, the tears rolling down her cheeks, "all the cattle are dead."

Mouth dropping open, Jasper looked but could not speak.

"Let me loose," said Dixon. "I can help."

"You?" Jasper, having found his voice, pulled out the empty Adams revolver from inside his waistband. "This was that old man's back in the camp we were at. You killed him and you took it."

"It's true I took it, but he was already dead."

"You expect me to believe that?"

"You can believe what the hell you like, it's the truth."

"So what were you doing visiting him in the middle of the night?"

"More whisky. He'd left me the jug but there wasn't no more than a mouthful left. I went to him to ask if he had any more, and there he was, dead. I didn't think it would do any harm by taking the gun."

"You lying scoundrel, you killed him. Murdered him."

"What, for a goddamned gun? And what was it I wanted it for, eh? To kill all of you in your beds? I needed a gun, I have always had one. Without one, I am vulnerable, afraid. I'm a lawman, you half-wit, and I—"

Jasper crossed the two or three steps separating them and struck Dixon back-handed across the face. The blow snapped Dixon's head sharply to the right and he gasped, squeezing his eyes shut, taking a moment to recover.

"*Liar*," spat Jasper.

"Prove it," said Dixon, swinging his head around to face his accuser once again. He licked up a dribble of blood from the side of his mouth.

"I don't need to."

"Then shoot me, you bastard."

"*Shoot* you? I'm not like you – I'm a God-fearing man."

"So what in the hell are you gonna do, Jasper?"

"I'm gonna keep you tethered and when we get to Salt Lake, I'll see you hang for what you did."

"Yeah, well…" Dixon chuckled and nodded over to where Arabella tended her stricken family, all of them laid out in the dirt, all of them curled up, rolling, moaning, bodily fluids oozing out of them in foul, stinking rivulets of filth, uncontrolled, seemingly endless. "By the looks of them I doubt any of us will make Salt Lake."

"God will protect us."

Dixon shook his head, did the best he could to make himself comfortable, and closed his eyes to try to find some semblance of sleep.

The following morning, when Dixon woke shivering so much from the cold his teeth rattled, he saw the prophetic truth of his words. They were all dead and Arabella, sitting beside them, quietly weeping, her world destroyed in the space of a few hours, stared into nothingness.

A shadow fell over him. It was Constance, Jasper's eldest child. She was crying. "What are we going to do?"

"Bury them."

"I meant about you."

"Ask your pa, he's the one with all the answers."

"Pa's dead."

She dropped down beside Dixon and worked away at the ropes binding him with a knife. Rupert's efforts at tying up the Marshal proved their worth as she sawed away at the bonds, tiny grunts coming from the back of her throat with the effort. As the last strand parted, Dixon instantly rubbed his wrists, and looked at her. She couldn't have been more than fourteen. "What the hell do you mean *dead*?"

She brushed away the sweat from her brow with the sleeve of her stained dress, looked to the ground and shuddered. "He died in the night."

"But ... " He placed his hands on her shoulders. "Wait, he didn't appear sick – not yesterday when he was talking to me."

"It happened before. Two years ago. It's his heart." She sniffed loudly. "*Was* his heart."

Dixon fell back against the wheel. "Holy damn."

"Rupert says we should take just the one wagon from now on – our wagon. The horses seem good thus far, and when we have laid everyone in the ground, we will continue."

She continued in this vein, words tumbling out of her, most of them making little sense. Dixon switched off but kept his eyes locked on her face, knowing this was her way of coping. By keeping herself busy, making plans and arrangements, she could keep her mind off the enormity of the situation. So he sat and he waited, and Constance talked until she could talk no more.

And when she stopped and she noticed his face, she broke down. He held her like that, her sobs soaking into his shirt, for as long as needed.

Dixon gently guided the wagon away from their final resting place. Arabella sat beside him, face a perfect mask of grief, eyes still and lifeless, mouth a thin blue line. It was as if some unseen hands had wrung out every last drop of goodness from her soul, leaving her dried up, empty. More than once he attempted to offer a comforting word, but received no response. In the end, he gave up.

That night he unhitched the horses tied up at the back of their wagon, the ones which once pulled Morris and his family across the prairie. He watched them trot off into the murky stillness and Constance came up alongside him. "Should I make us all something to eat?"

He looked at her. A young woman, grown so much older these last few days, the heavy weight of responsibility forcing her to mature beyond what was natural. She had seen more than most.

"Arabella is not well," he said simply.

"You think she has it?"

"Perhaps, although she would be showing signs already. No, it's something more. She's died inside."

"Yes. I held Rupert all through the night. He is strong, but ... We have lost so much. I'm thinking that maybe we should turn back."

He blinked at her. "But you're so close."

"I know, but it was always Pa's dream to go there, to meet up with Brigham Young. Now, I am asking the Lord 'why'. To come all this way, to suffer so many deprivations, and all for what?"

"Come with me to Twin Buttes. I know people there. We could set up, make a home. A family."

"Are you serious?"

"I am."

"But we are not your kin."

He smiled, put his arm around her shoulders and held her close. "You are now."

After they ate, Constance took the chance and went over to speak with Arabella, who sat on a rock staring into the night. Dixon washed out the plates and saw Rupert playing with the empty Dean revolver.

The boy caught him looking. He hefted the revolver in his hand and his voice came heavy, dull. Flat. "Did you kill the old man to take this?"

"No. Like I told your Pa, the old man was dead already."

"It's heavy. Have you no more cartridges?"

"No. We have no more powder." He tapped the Navy Colt in his belt. "Five shots is all we have. There's another in your Pa's carbine, and the one Mr. Morris had. It's in the wagon. A total of seven shots. If we come across a bunch of Bannocks or Utes, we'd be dead."

His eyes grew wide with terror. In the ghostly, shimmering light of the campfire he took on the look of a demon, deep shadows cast from his nose and cheekbones across a ruddy face.

"Don't fret none, Rupert. Once they take several casualties, they'll run off. They always do. All they want are the horses, maybe some food."

"But if they take the horses we'll—"

"They won't take anything." Dixon let out his breath slowly, wishing he had never mentioned anything about Indians. Since the shooting at the river, he had not spotted a single sign of any more braves, but they were deep in Ute territory now and danger lurked in every shadow, in every fold of the land. "We'll be just fine."

"Connie says you are meaning to take us to Twin Buttes."

"Yes. We'll be safer there."

"I hope it's true." He lifted up the revolver. "Can this be my gun, when we get there?"

"I don't see why not. It's a point and shoot. I'll teach you."

"You're good with guns."

"I am."

"If cholera was a person, I'd shoot him dead."

Dixon turned away and choked down the tears welling up from inside. These people were the closest to family as any he had ever known. As he lay down and curled himself up in a tight ball, sleep did not come, despite exhaustion withering every sinew, every joint.

He felt rather than heard Constance sitting down beside him.

"She won't speak."

Rolling over, he looked up at her. "Maybe when we reach town, she might come to terms with what's happened."

"Maybe. But I'm not so sure."

He reached out and brushed her arm. She smiled, got up and went over to where Rupert lay next to the wagon.

The fire crackled, the stars shone and from out of the night came the gentle sobs of Arabella.

In the morning, as Dixon stretched out his bones, he looked across at the still sleeping children and smiled. The campfire was now nothing more than grey ashes and he set to clearing them away to make room for fresh kindling. Putting a handful of coffee beans into the old, beaten up metal pot, he scanned the camp and frowned. Arabella was not there. Gripped by a sudden sense of foreboding, he stood up, bringing out the Navy. Easing back the hammer, he carefully walked towards the rock where he saw her sitting the night before. His eyes travelled to the fringe of sagebrush and the trees beyond.

He saw her there.

Hanging from a nearby branch.

For a long time he could not speak, nor move. Only when Constance joined him did he manage to trawl up enough strength to say, "Now we really do not have any reason to go on."

Her hand slipped into his and they both stood and watched the body gently swinging to and fro.

Twenty-Five

Not so many years ago, the town of Fairweather pulsated with the sound of a thousand voices, children laughing and running in the streets, families seeking a new life, businesses thriving, saloons full of prospectors and pilgrims. In those days, Ben Magee ruled with an iron fist. He banned the carrying of firearms within the town limits, patrolled the streets ensuring drunks and other trouble-makers were dealt with quickly and efficiently and stood as judge and jury in disputes.

Now all of that was but a distant memory.

Located in a narrow valley, rough-hewn hills forming a natural boundary between it and the wide, open spaces, the town was a mix of wooden frame shacks and small, false fronted commercial buildings. A few old, mangy looking mules stood outside the tired looking saloon. Many buildings stood silent, most boarded up, including the bank and the hotel. A blacksmith worked at his forge, and a hostler, chewing on a piece of straw, sat close by, working at an old saddle. Both men looked up as Simms and Cross walked their horses up to the saloon and dismounted.

"You boys need to call in and see the sheriff," called over the hostler. "You have to hand in them there irons."

Simms screwed up his mouth and nodded without making a reply. He turned to the saloon. "If you go on inside, I'll wander round back."

"You certain this is the correct way to go about this?"

"Until I set my eyes on Magee, I don't know what to expect. He might be a wizened up old man, or he might be hell-on-wheels. I'm not about to take any chances."

Cross grunted and stepped up onto the boardwalk. He rotated his shoulders and went through the saloon entrance.

Waiting for only a few seconds, Simms crossed over to the two men. The blacksmith laid down a pair of tongs and stood up to his full, impressive height. Like most in his profession, he was big across the chest and shoulders, his arms solid and powerful, ample belly straining against his leather apron. He ran a forearm across his sweating brow and studied Simms with narrow, intelligent looking eyes.

The Pinkerton gave a slight nod. "Where would the sheriff be?"

The big man thought, then shrugged. "It's early. More than likely at his home." He pointed down the main drag. "Two blocks on the left. Big house, twin-fronted. There's usually a buggy outside. He likes to ride in his buggy."

"You didn't read the sign as you came in," said the hostler, still working away at the saddle leather.

"Nope. I think maybe the wind blew it down."

"We don't get wind here." The hostler looked up, thin, weasel-faced, thinning brown hair. He flashed a grin, exposing the large gap in his front teeth.

Simms smiled. "Except out of your ass, maybe."

The big blacksmith puffed up his chest, a dangerous look coming over his face. "Hey, now hold on there, stranger—"

He got no further as, from through the swing doors of the saloon, Cross exploded into view, flying through the air to land face down in the dirt. He lay there, stunned for a moment. Shaking his head, he levered himself up by his palms and sat dazed whilst behind him a big hulking brute appeared, fists clenched, foam flecking his lips, eyes wide with maniacal glee.

"Oh my," muttered the hostler in a low voice, "that'll be Eugene Neilson. Not a man to tangle with."

Simms grunted and folded his arms and peered across the street. "I'd say he is bigger than you, Mr. Blacksmith."

"He is that."

Stomping down the steps, which buckled dangerously under his weight, Eugene reached out with one mighty paw and lifted Cross to his feet. He slammed a big, heavy right into the Federal agent's guts, folding him up like a penknife, then swung his knee up into his jaw, pitching him backwards into the ground again. Writhing, Cross didn't look as if he'd be getting up again this time, so Simms decided he should intervene. He wandered across the street, peeling back his coat to reveal the holstered Navy.

"Friend," he said, his eyes holding Eugene's, "I think it's time to stop."

"The hell it is." The big man's accent seemed foreign, not unlike Simms's old friend Martinson back in the town of Bovey. The thought brought with it a tiny stab of nostalgia as a flutter of memories danced around in his head. Pulling in a breath, he oppressed the images. "Friend, I'm asking you kindly – step back."

"Fuck you, whoever you are, I'm gonna kill him."

"No you ain't." Simms's hand curled around the butt of the Colt. "You've done enough. Whatever he has done, you've paid him in full. Now back off."

Two more men, considerably smaller, emerged from the saloon. They were young, work clothes stained with dirt and sweat, their faces grimy, their teeth, those they had, gleaming with anticipation.

"Mister, you have no right to be toting a gun round here," said one of them as he moved closer. "This here bastard got to talking to us about Sheriff Magee and Eugene, he took exception."

"That's right," said the second man, "then he cussed at Eugene and Eugene don't like that."

"I don't like cussing."

Simms drew a breath and let it come out in a loud blast. He didn't think he should point out the hypocrisy of the big man's words, having himself only that moment burst out an expletive of his own. "Well, if that is all this is, can we just call it quits now?" He looked down at Cross who moaned and rolled over onto his front.

"I won't say what he called Eugene, but nobody talks to him like that."

"No sir."

"No sir," echoed Eugene. "I'm gonna kill him."

He reached down and Simms's gun came up in a blur. "You move another muscle, boy, and I'll put you down for good."

Something pricked between the Pinkerton's shoulder blades, an eerie sixth-sense causing him to turn.

Three men strode across the street, determination etched into every fibre of their bodies, faces set hard and grim.

The look of men well acquainted with violence and, in particular, the one in the lead, whose voice sizzled with confrontation, "I'm saying you is a mite too confident there, mister."

The others froze at the sound of the voice, the two younger men growing pale, Eugene raising his great bear paws in supplication. Only Simms remained outwardly calm as he studied the short yet bulky individual in shirtsleeves and dungarees, bare-headed, sporting a Colt Dragoon at his hip standing before him. Close behind were the other two men, wearing typical ranch hand garb, muskets in their hands. Summing up the situation with a quick scan, the leader stuck his thumbs inside his belt and puffed out his chest. "My name is Ben Magee, sheriff of this here town, and I'll be asking you to hand over your guns."

"I'm a Pinkerton Detective," said Simms, "this here is a Federal agent, down from Washington. We're on government business and we'll truck no interference. Not from you or anyone."

Magee ran his tongue over his top lip, eying Simms's revolver keenly. "Mister, you may think you have the drop on us, but my two boys will shoot you dead if you don't follow my laws."

"I'll kill them both before you can clean your holster, Magee. Then you too. So back down."

"Sheriff," squawked on of the two with muskets, "he looks like he means business."

"Shut up, Henderson," said Magee out of the corner of his mouth. "Mister, you'd do well to follow my orders."

"And you'd do well to tell your boys to drop their guns."

With the impasse reached nobody moved, some daring not to even breathe. Magee's eyes flickered, for the first time uncertainty developing in his features.

Simms stood, the Colt ready, aware of the three behind him and the three in front. He had five shots. Already his mind had gone through the permutations. He'd shoot Henderson first, then Magee. Put the second musketeer in the ground and the others would run. Eugene probably wouldn't and Simms knew he'd need at least two shots to put the big man down before he brought out the Smith and Wesson. By then, it would all be over. He smiled. "Magee, this ain't ending well unless you tell your boys to drop their guns."

"And you ain't telling me what to do in my own town."

A groan from the ground and Cross sat up, holding his face, the blood splashing down his shirt front. "What in the hell hit me."

"I did," growled Eugene.

Shaking his head, Cross climbed to his feet, swaying slightly, and took in the situation. "Oh shit."

"I'm gonna count to three," said Magee.

Simms's voice came cold and unfaltering. "Before you make it, you'll be dead."

The silence stretched out, the world freezing solid, nothing moving, every insect, bird and anything else that lived and breathed waiting in expectation of what would happen next.

"Look," said Cross easily, dabbing at his nose with his neckerchief, "let's say we all go over to your office, Sheriff and talk this through. There is no need for gunplay." He pulled out a small black wallet from his side pocket and flipped it open. Pinned to the inside was a gold shield, "I am who Mr. Simms says – a Federal agent, with orders from the Government itself to carry out my orders without hindrance." Nodding towards Eugene, standing there with his breath snorting out of his nostrils like a steam train, he gave a grim smile. "My apologies, big feller, if I offended you – it was not my intention." He felt his jaw. "And if I'd known what reaction my words would incur, I surely would not have spoken the way I did. Forgive me."

Eugene threw up his hands, exasperated. "Well hell … I guess I can accept what you say, but I was mighty offended."

"Yes. And again, I ask you to accept my sincerest apologies."

Grunting, Eugene shot a glance towards Magee. "Seems reasonable."

Magee blew out a breath. "Well, seems like I have no choice but to accept the status quo, Mister Federal Agent. But be warned, as soon as you have informed me what in the hell you want, you are leaving my town without argument. You understand?"

"We understand," said Cross and slipped his badge back into his pocket. "Detective Simms, please reholster your weapon."

Simms glanced over to the two with muskets. "Boys, you shoulder your rifles real easy, then I'll comply with your boss's wishes."

"Do it," snapped Magee.

The men indeed complied and Simms put away the Navy. He looked to Cross, who gave him a wink, then they all moved in behind Magee and went down the street to his office.

Twenty-Six

Four riders came out of the swirling heat haze at an easy canter. Martinson, working on a new set of fences, paused, pushed his hat back and dragged his shirtsleeve across his brow. He'd toiled since early morning, hoping to do as much as he could before the sun's fury became too much. Now, close to finishing for the day, he frowned as he peered towards the approaching strangers. It was unusual for people to pass this way, unless someone from Bovey had news for Simms. Everyone knew Simms was away on government business so who these strangers were or what they might want the Swede had no way of telling. But something about them caused the hairs across his shoulders to prickle. He looked across to the cabin. White Dove would be inside, or perhaps out back. She often spent time in the small coral, extending it, readying it for more horses. If he called her, she would not hear. He wondered if he was being overly cautious but when he laid eyes on the men again, with their guns tied down to the hips, he knew there was something very wrong.

They came to a halt and one of the men, wearing a black tailcoat, pushed his horse slightly forward as the others sat and stared.

"'Morning," said the man, touching the brim of his hat, "it sure is a hot one."

"That it is." Martinson's eyes roamed across the other men, their black, lifeless eyes peering back out at him from stone-cold faces. The hand he brought up to his mouth trembled. "What can I do for you gentlemen?"

The man smiled and dipped into the breast pocket of his coat to bring out a pair of spectacles. He perched them on his nose and produced a paper from an inside pocket. He unfolded it and read through the words as if for the first time. "Mr. Simms, I have here a bill of sale, one whose terms I believe you will find most agreeable."

"Bill of sale?" He gave a half smile, looking at each man in turn, "Bill of sale for what?"

The man offered the paper. "Read it through, Mr. Simms. It's all here."

"I'd prefer it if you told me."

"Ah." The man nodded, as if understanding something unsaid. "Well, putting it briefly, Mr. Simms, this is an offer for your land." He swept his hand in a grandiose manner from left to right. "*All* your land. Times are changing, Mr. Simms, and they are changing fast. With the gold and silver almost all petered out, investors are looking at other avenues to increase their wealth. Land is now seen as one of the most profitable. This is good, prime meadow, Mr. Simms, and is perfect for my clients' needs. We will give you above market price."

"And the ranch?"

"I beg your pardon?"

"The ranch," Martinson turned and pointed towards the cabin. "What becomes of that?"

"Well, I'm sure ... Mr. Simms, you will have more than enough money to purchase another plot."

"I see." Martinson swallowed hard.

"It's a good offer, Mr. Simms – the best you'll get."

"I'm sure it is."

The man smiled, looked at the paper again, "Listen, no offence, but you can make your mark at the bottom. I will signature it as being your name."

"I can read. And write."

"Ah. Forgive me, I assumed you could not."

"I can. I am good at figures too."

The man peered over the top of his spectacles. "Mr. Simms, I'm not quite sure if you fully understand what I am offering here. It's a good deal, one which you will—"

"Oh, I'm sure it is a good deal, Mister …?"

"Burrows. Ernest Burrows. I'm a lawyer representing the Moss and Maine Cattle Company of Wyoming."

"Wyoming? That's a long way from here."

"Like I said – new opportunities. Now then, Mr. Simms, if you'd like to sign we can—"

"I am not Simms."

Burrows did a double-take, even checked the paper again, a deep frown developing on his face. "I'm sorry, but I was under the impression a Mr. R Simms held claim to this land."

"That he does. But I am not he."

The frown again. Burrows shifted in his saddle, giving his companions the briefest of looks. He returned to Martinson, forcing a smile. "Well perhaps you could—" He stopped, his mouth falling open. One of the men behind whistled softly, another hissed, "Oh my."

Martinson turned and saw White Dove stepping out from the side ranch house. She wore a light blue checked shirt tied at the midriff, her skin taut and bronzed above the waistband of her work trousers. Her body, exposed at the neck and forearms, glistened with sweat, her blue-black hair pulled back in a tight ponytail to reveal a face tanned, smooth, and beautiful. In her arms, she cradled a Halls carbine. "Simms is away on business," she said, her voice calm, untroubled.

Burrows coughed, gave a slight smile. "So you must be—"

"When he returns, you can talk to him."

"I see. And when, er, might that be my good lady?"

"When he returns."

"Yes, I understand, but …" He gave a short sigh. "This paper has to be signed. You can do it."

"It is Simms's ranch. You must deal with him."

"My clients are mighty impatient."

Behind him the other three urged their hoses forward until they were lined up alongside the lawyer.

Martinson held up a hand. "Mr. Burrows, any document we sign will not be legal and will not hold up in court if there is a counter-claim. Simms is the owner of this land." He watched the way the men's hands hovered close to their guns. "No amount of intimidation is going to alter that fact."

Chewing around the inside of his mouth, Burrows took a long time considering Martinson's words. At last, he blew out a tremendous sigh, folded up the paper and slipped it back into his pocket. "This is somewhat disappointing. I shall return in two days. If Mr. Simms has not returned by then, you will both sign as his representatives. I shall have a court order which states your signatures will be legally binding."

"I'm not sure if Simms would agree to that."

Tilting his head, Burrows's smile widened, "Well, he's not going to have much choice."

"I'd call that a threat, Mr. Burrows."

"Call it what you will – you have two days."

"When you come back," said White Dove evenly, "you'd best bring more men." She shifted the carbine. "You will need them."

"So now who is making threats?"

"It's no threat," interjected Martinson, "it's just the way it is. Simms ain't gonna sign over this land, Mr. Burrows. You tell your clients that. Whilst you're at it, I'd make some inquiries about Simms, if I were you. With what you'll find, you might think twice before you come around here again."

Burrows doffed his hat, then turned his horse, the others moving in behind him, save for one, rangy looking individual, who considered Martinson through narrowing eyes. "Two days," he said before moving up to the others.

They made off across the plain much faster than they arrived, the horses throwing up clouds of dust as they disappeared into the distance.

"They mean trouble," said Martinson.

"Yes. I shall ride over to Deep Water. We may need help."

Twenty-Seven

The town was much as he remembered it. People scurried around, suffering from the heat, especially the women in their bonnets and trailing skirts. Easing in the reins and guiding the team towards the livery stable, Dixon kept his eyes straight head, conscious some townsfolk might recognise him.

Beside him, Constance shook her head. "This is not what I expected.
"

"Oh? And what were you expecting? Streets paved with gold?"

She snapped her head towards him. "Mr. Dixon, you are uncouth. I was merely expressing my disappointment. This is nothing like the towns we were told about out east."

"Well, they sell you their stories, Connie, to get you out here. You must have paid good money for the information."

"Mr. Morris would have done all that. We saw the hoardings, studied the route. As far as I know, the only money Mr. Morris handed over was for a map and some firearms."

Dixon grunted, patting the Navy in his waistband. "Which reminds me, I need ball and powder."

"Where are we going to stay?" asked Rupert, poking his head out from inside the wagon.

"I know of a little place which will do us until I can find something more permanent."

"Our desire was to go to Salt Lake," said Constance.

"I ain't about to dessert you right here, right now. Once we is settled, then we can inquire if any other pilgrims are heading that way."

"Then you will accompany us?"

Dixon studied her face, the hope written in her eyes. His heart lurched for a brief moment and he looked away. "Connie, it was never my intention to go all the way to Salt Lake. This is where I intended to come, and here I am."

"But we have no one else."

Dixon let out a long sigh and eased the wagon into the livery stable yard. He eyed a bow-legged old man stumbling towards him and said, "I have to sort this out, Connie. Then we'll wander over to an eating place I know, get ourselves some food. I'll need to pay the sheriff a call, as well as get some merchandise from the store."

"Including gunpowder for your revolvers? Yes, I understand what you mean by merchandise, Mr. Dixon."

Dixon ignored her and jumped down, running his hand along the nearest horse as the liveryman stepped up close.

"I'll need these animals brushed down, fed and rested. Then another horse for a day or two. If you have one."

"I do, mister. Have you the money to pay?"

Dixon arched a single eyebrow, dipped into his trouser pocket and handed over two silver coins. "That'll cover it, and a lot more besides. Have that horse saddled within the hour."

"You are well used to giving orders," said Constance, clambering down from the wagon seat.

Dixon helped her as Rupert jumped down from the back and came up, all eager, rubbing his hands together. "A real Western town!"

"It ain't nothing to get excited about," said Dixon, but he couldn't help but smile. "I'll take you over to the eating house, then we'll—"

"Where did you get the money?"

Dixon went to speak, but then held the words back. To his mind, Constance never seemed to miss a trick. He took a breath, "I'm not going to lie to you Connie – I took it from your father's belongings."

"And Mr. Morris's too, I shouldn't wonder."

"Yes. What else was I to do, just leave it with them?"

"He's right, Connie," said Rupert.

"It would have been nice to have been informed, is all."

"Well, my apologies for that, but I didn't really have the time to—"

"I knew it was you as soon as I saw this old Prairie Schooner ambling by," came a voice from somewhere close behind.

Dixon stopped, his eyes locked on Constance. He noted the bemused expression on her face as she looked over his shoulder. He let out a long breath, put his thumbs into his belt and turned.

A burly man stood there, feet planted apart, gripping the butt of the revolver at his side. Slightly behind him stood two younger men, their guns already drawn. They appeared edgy, eyes darting this way and that, breathing through their mouths, sweat on their brow.

"Hello Silas."

"I thought you were dead," said Silas, never allowing his eyes to leave Dixon's. The air crackled with tension. Rupert gave an involuntary moan.

"Not yet."

"When Simms rode out to old Dan's camp, I felt sure he'd finish you."

"Seems you was wrong."

"Does he know?"

"Simms? Nope, he doesn't know. But he will."

Silas smiled, gesturing to the children, without lowering his gaze. "Who might these be?"

"Orphans."

"Well hell, Dixon, don't that beat all. Who murdered their parents – you?"

"Who *is* this individual?" asked Constance, her voice tremulous. Rupert pressed himself into her and she put her arm protectively around him.

"I am the town sheriff, miss. This man here has certain questions to answer."

"What sort of questions?"

"Pertaining to the death of a young girl – Dan Stoakes's daughter; Sarah Milligan."

"That's bull," spat Dixon. "She died of fever, and you know it – you saw her, goddamn it."

"Don't cuss, Mr. Dixon."

Dixon gave Constance a withering look. "This bastard will have me swinging from the nearest tree before the sun sets, Connie. I'll not worry about invoking the Lord's wrath on me right this moment."

"Well you should."

Silas emitted a loud roar, "Hell's bells, she has your measure, Dixon. Maybe you should marry her, *if* you survive the trial."

"Shut your fat old mouth. There ain't gonna be no trial, you half-wit, 'cause I ain't done nothin'."

"I think Simms and the circuit judge will decide that, Dixon. Now, you hand over your gun and let's go talk in my office. My two boys have you covered and you'll be dead before you can spit if you make a play."

"What does he mean, Mr. Dixon? Is what he says true – you had a hand in that poor girl's murder?"

"She died of fever," Dixon said through clenched teeth.

Silas breathed hard. "Then why did Simms seek out your trail, eh? He had something on you, I know that much."

"You know nothing, Silas. Basically all you do is sit behind your big old desk, getting fatter and slower by the second, whilst the real lawmen in this Territory do all the hard work."

"That's a damned lie, you spineless sonofabitch. "

"Only one spineless round here, Silas, is you. You ain't nothing's without your backup, not that they is up to much by the look of 'em."

"Well, we got the drop on you, Dixon."

"Hardly. I reckon them boys are pissin' in their pants right now, same as you, you big hulking sack of shit."

Silas's face grew redder, his jowls quivering as he raged, "Shut the hell up, Dixon! You know nothing about nothing."

"I know you is a cowardly fat bastard who couldn't lift his own pecker, never mind his fists."

With a roar, Silas charged forward, hands out to seize Dixon and tear him apart.

If he'd have made it, things might have turned out differently, but Dixon was moving faster than Silas could ever have imagined. Skipping nimbly to the side, Dixon's foot cracked into Silas's ankle whilst his hands took hold of the lurching sheriff by the lapels, twisting and turning him in a narrow arc. With his forearm clamped around his windpipe, his other hand deftly lifted the sheriff's gun from its holster and aimed it unerringly towards the two deputies.

"Boys," breathed Dixon, "you put the guns down and get on home to mama; me and uncle Silas here are gonna do some talking."

Silas struggled in Dixon's grip, which only caused the forearm to tighten still further. He managed to rattle, "Do it boys," then winced as Dixon stuck the barrel of the gun into his temple. "Do it *now*."

As the two deputies dropped their guns and moved away, Rupert took up a little jig, laughing at the top of his voice. "Hot dang, it's just like in them stories pa used to bring home from the newsstand."

"You quieten down," snapped Constance and flounced over to the guns. Picking them up, she hefted them in her hands, looking askance at Dixon. "I've a good mind to shoot you, Mr. Dixon."

"I reckon you could do it," said Dixon. "What do you say, Silas?"

"I reckon you're a dead man as soon as you set me free."

Dixon chuckled, released his grip and swung the sheriff round to face him. Silas immediately set up rubbing his throat, eyes settling on Dixon's hand, and the gun in particular. "You left handed now?"

Dixon grinned and held up his right, with the first two fingers missing. "Simms shot 'em off. He is as quick as lightning, that man."

"Pity he didn't finish you."

"He tried. Left me to bleed out down at Dan's camp. Much to my amazement, Dan wasn't dead and helped me to recover."

"You have the luck of the Devil, I'll say that for you."

Another smile and Dixon nodded towards Constance. "I'd put those things away if I were you, sweetheart, then go on over to the eating house just down the street from the saloon. I'll be there directly." He lifted Silas's gun, "I have enough ammunition to see me through so I won't be needing the merchant store."

Constance stood for a moment, screwing up her mouth, considering what to do. Rupert went up to her and tugged at her skirt. "Come on, sis. I haven't eaten a good meal for days. Let's leave Mr. Dixon to his business."

"It's the subject of that business which worries me." She moved away, throwing the guns into the back of the wagon, nodding to the livery man who stood and stared, as he had done throughout the entire exchange.

"Well," said Dixon when Constance and her brother were safely out of earshot, "you and me have some talking to do, Silas."

"There's nothing you can say which is of any interest to me. You're a murdering son of whore and I won't rest until I see you swinging from the end of a rope."

"You know I told you old Dan saved me? Found me unconscious, close to death? He patched me up, sewed up the worst of my wounds and nursed me back to health."

"What the hell has that got to do with anything?"

"Hardly the actions of a loving father towards the man who'd murdered his daughter."

Silas pursed his lips. "Perhaps he didn't know."

"Simms shot me at the camp, Silas. The same camp where Sarah died." He tilted his head. "Think about it."

"All right, but even if he didn't suspect you doesn't mean you didn't do it."

"You know how hollow that sounds, Silas?"

"As hollow as a dead, rotten tree trunk."

Both men turned as the livery man stepped out from behind the covered wagon. "As an impartial observer," he said, "I gotta say, I don't think your accusations hold much credence, Sheriff."

"You keep out of this, Augustus. None of this has anything to do with you."

Augustus shrugged. "I'm just saying what a lot of people will think, Silas. You is up for re-election come June. I'd think well on that if I were you."

"We're gonna stay down at the camp for a while," said Dixon quickly before Silas could come with a suitable response to the old man's words. "Now we have everything smoothed over," he relaxed his grip on the sheriff's gun, keeping his forefinger through the trigger guard, and let it swing upside down. He thrust out his hand towards Silas, "I reckon we can all sleep soundly in our bed without fear of being assaulted in the night."

Silas grunted and took back the gun. He dropped it back into its holster. "I want you out of this town Dixon ... Just as soon as you are able."

Dixon brought his forefinger to his brow in a mock salute and watched the sheriff waddle away. Only then did he allow himself to relax.

"Seems like you owe me, Mister."

Dixon smiled at the old livery man. "What was your name again?"

"Augustus."

"Well, Augustus," he reached inside his waistcoat pocket and pulled out a thin roll of creased up dollar bills. He peeled off two of them and passed them over.

Augustus took them and considered them greedily for a moment. "I reckon keeping your neck out of the noose is worth a lot more than two dollars, *Marshal* Dixon."

"How in the hell do you know my—"

"I keep my head down and my ears close to the ground. Not much passes me by. I'll call it fifty."

Dixon gasped. "I ain't got that sort of money."

"Then my advice would be for you to find it, because if you don't ..." He shook his head and, cackling like some wizened old crone, he moved across to the horses and began to unhitch them.

For the first time for many, many days, Dixon felt the ice-cold grip of fear seizing him, squeezing tight.

Twenty-Eight

Crossing the street towards the saloon, which bore a hoarding announcing rooms were available, the two lawmen neither spoke nor looked at one another. The meeting with Magee had not only proved fruitful, but enlightening beyond their dreams, causing them both to reflect deeply on what the information they received.

Received was probably not the word to describe how Simms had extracted from Magee what he knew. Cross, standing in the corner, preferred to gaze out of the window, closing his ears to the sound of Simms's fists cracking ribs and chipping teeth.

Entering the office, Simms had motioned for Cross to bar the door. Magee, eyes wide, held up both his hands. "I'm not sure what you're hoping to discover, but you ain't got no—"

Simms silenced him with a thundering left hook to the temple, which dumped him unceremoniously to his knees. His face came up, lips trembling, eyes rolling in his head, muttering, "Holy shit, don't—"

Lifting him by the throat, Simms slammed a right fist into the man's ample gut, supported him in both hands and butted him square in the nose, sending him reeling across his desk, blood spewing from his ruined face.

"Now then," said Simms, taking off his hat, then his coat. "I'm going to be real nice with you, Sheriff Magee. As long as you tell me what I need to know."

For an answer, Magee groaned and rolled over onto his side, muttering something about the law and justice. Chuckling, Simms went around the desk and pulled out the drawers, one by one, rifling through the contents. He brought out a sheaf of papers and flicked through them. There were one or two telegrams, along with a batch of wanted posters waiting for Magee to pin them up outside the office. Quickly reading the telegrams, Simms then sat down on Magee's swivel chair and studied each of the posters in turn.

"To my mind," said Simms, leaning back, whilst not an arm's stretch away from him Magee lolled over the desk top, "these here boys," he laid down three of the posters face up in front of him, "you knew them a mite better than you should. They escaped from prison and I was *instructed* to apprehend them. This fella," he tapped the hastily sketched image of Brewster, "told me the whole sorry affair. So, *you* are going to tell me exactly what you know about these boys and what your part in this whole stinking plan was. Then my good friend over there, who works for the United States government, is going to bring to justice the man responsible for the killing of Senator Bowen."

It took several more punches before Magee gave everything up. Afterwards, Simms hauled the slobbering mess of what used to be the sheriff into the tiny cell and clanged the door shut.

Now, in the saloon, the two lawmen waited at a corner table, eagerly waiting for the waitress to bring them food. Cross, head down, idly moved his knife and fork together, tapping them in a steady, almost hypnotic beat.

"When Magee mentioned that feller's name, the mastermind if you like – the one called Moss – you acted as if you knew him."

Simms blew out a breath, "I know *of* him. He's a land-grabber, from what I can ascertain."

"He's more than that – he's the man responsible for Bowen's death."

"We still don't know why. We got a lot out of Magee – about the hiring of Brewster and the others, how Porter sent me that telegram, pertaining to be from my office in Chicago, ordering me to track them down and bring them in. Then to have us all killed by Porter's men."

"Who are now also dead."

"Accidents happen."

"Those two gunned down at Bridger were not the result of any accident, Simms. You told Faulkner and me you didn't have an accomplice. You lied."

"Deep Water is my friend – he watches my back."

"Then he tracks down Porter and pegs him out in the prairie."

"We may never have found him if that hadn't happened."

"You're too free and easy with the law, Simms. That confession you beat out of Magee, it won't hold up in court. He'll deny everything."

Simms shrugged. "By then it'll all be wrapped up, so who gives a damn."

"Hell, Simms, I'm not comfortable with any of this."

"Cross, sometimes expediency is the only way – we haven't got time to be dilly-dallying with these people."

"Even so, Simms. What you did was illegal."

"Illegal?" He leaned forward, eyes narrowing, "This ain't no Sunday Fourth of July party, Cross. This is war, pure and simple. This bastard Moss sets out to kill Bowen, and he does so. Then he ties up all the pieces in the hope of diverting attention from him by shaming it all up as a robbery."

"He didn't tie it up tight enough – he never expected you to beat the information out of Magee. To tell you truth, neither did I."

"Don't play the self-righteous holier-than-thou bullshit with me, Cross. I did what I had to do, and we're in a much better state now than we were before."

"Are we? We still don't know why Moss wanted Bowen dead. And what if something happens to Magee? We won't have a shred of evidence to put this Moss character away."

"We have Porter. He'll squawk like a bird once he knows Magee has rolled over."

"You think so?"

"I do."

Simms leaned back again as the waitress came with their food. Simms nodded his thanks and noticed a man talking feverishly to the barman on the other side of the counter. As he listened, the barman's face grew drawn, nervous. He cast a quick glance towards Simms and looked away, startled. The man leaned into him, speaking rapidly before disappearing through a back door. Shifting in his chair, Simms pondered whether or not to move over and ask the barman what the problem was all about – because there sure was a problem. He could see it in the way the barman looked around shiftily, polishing glasses already clean for something to do

"This looks good," said Cross, cutting into the Pinkerton's thoughts.

Simms looked again at his plate; the rib steak was enormous, the beans and tomatoes cooked to perfection. For the moment, he put aside his developing sense of unease and licked his lips. "I don't think I've eaten this well since leaving Chicago."

Cross laughed and they both attacked their food with gusto.

Later, having washed down their dinner with a glass of cold, palatable beer, the barman sidled up to them and Simms measured him with a penetrating stare.

"Gentlemen," the barman began, looking from one to the other, "I'm afraid the rooms we had prepared for you are not up to standard. We had a storm not so long ago, and rainwater got in through the roof and we—"

"So what you're saying," cut in Simms sharply, "is you don't have a room, despite telling us you did."

"No, no, I, er, the thing is. . ." he smiled self-consciously, "We *do* have a room – a good one too."

"So what's the problem?"

"No problem, it's just that the room is in the bunkhouse, out back."

"Is it clean?" demanded Cross, leaning forward, suddenly serious.

"Oh yes, it's clean. Hot dang, I wouldn't be explaining the situation if it wasn't—"

Simms cut in, voice sounding harsh when he said, "And is that what the little scraggly fella was telling you about, just before?"

"*Scraggly fella*? Oh, you mean Samuel? Yes, he came to tell me he'd discovered your rooms were not up to our usual standard."

"But the bunkhouse is?" asked Cross again.

"Yes sir, it surely is."

"Well then," said Cross, sitting back and patting his stomach with both hands. "A good dinner, a cool beer, and a comfortable bed. Can't ask for much else, can we Simms."

But Simms wasn't listening. Instead, his eyes settled on scraggly Samuel who loitered close to the counter, shifty-eyed, nervous. The Pinkerton sighed and stood up. Level now with the barman, he looked deep into the man's eyes and saw something familiar.

Fear.

"How exactly is the room not up to your usual standards?"

The barman frowned. "Huh? I don't quite—"

"Samuel. He don't exactly look at ease with any of this."

"Oh, him ... " The barman chuckled. "He's fearful for his wife – it's her that prepares the room. He's thinking she might lose her job because of it. He's hoping you don't make any complaints."

That nervous, cackling laugh again.

Simms put his hands on the counter's edge and pushed himself away. "No. Not as long as the bunkhouse is as good as you say it is."

"Oh, it is." The barman winked. "I promise."

Nodding, Simms returned to his table. "Trouble?" asked Cross.

Simms shook his head, certain there would not be any trouble. At least, not until morning.

* * *

The room yawned hellish black as Simms sat bolt upright in his bed. He closed his eyes again for a few moments, struggling to gather his senses. The bunkhouse smelled of old straw and damp hay, but the beds were sturdy and clean, the sheets neatly pressed.

It was not any of this, which woke him with a start.

Breathing evenly next to him, Cross continued sleeping like a baby.

But something wasn't right.

Simms groped for the single oil lamp on the table next to the bed and turned it up. He always preferred to keep a lamp burning in strange places and he gave up a little prayer of thanks for doing so. As he lifted up the lamp, he saw it. Ghostly grey tendrils of smoke seeped beneath the bunkhouse door and crept like a living thing upwards across the walls. The smell of smoke caught at the back of his throat and now, as he gazed in disbelief, he saw the first flickers of flame lapping around the door's edges, glowing orange and yellow as they took hold of the tinder-dry walls.

Swinging out of bed, he crossed to the door, initial thoughts on pushing open the door and escaping. But as he drew closer the heat told him everything he needed to know – the flames beyond were too intense. Opening the doors would result in a sudden roar of fire and the entire building would ignite within seconds, trapping both of them inside.

He swung around and ran to Cross, shaking the Federal agent awake.

"What in the name of Good God Almighty are you—"

"We have to get out," rasped Simms, unable to keep the fear out of his voice. He took a look back at the door. There was no longer any need for the oil lamp, the flames licking upwards with terrifying rapidity, the door planking spitting and crackling as flames consumed the woodwork. Even as he watched, the fire spread to either side. Soon the flames would engulf all that part of the bunkhouse and them with it.

Simms looked up into the hayloft and the small hatch built into the upper wall. He gripped Cross by the shoulder, "We have to get up there, but we have to be quick."

Already the smoke was building, a thick, acrid blanket wafting upwards, clogging the air, causing both men to cough and splutter. Cross doubled up, fell out of bed, grabbing blindly for his gun and coat.

"No time for dressing," shouted Simms. Clad in only his long johns, he grabbed his gun belt from the bedpost and rushed over to the ladder leading to the hayloft. Without pausing, he ascended.

He was aware of noise outside, townsfolk no doubt woken by the fire. Mindless of that, with straw already smouldering, he ran across barefooted to the hayloft hatch and pushed it open.

A gun shot rang out, a lead ball streaking mere inches away from his head, forcing him to pull away from the open hatch.

"Jesus God," screamed Cross, looming up beside him, body-jarring coughs sending him into uncontrolled convulsions.

By now the fire blazed all along the downstairs walls, the noise of burning wood loud enough to drown any words. Simms, putting the back of his hand against his eyes, loosed off three shots into the night. Then he clambered out, hooking one leg over the sill, and prepared to jump.

Pieces of hot lead sang past him, but the time for hesitation was long gone. The heat and noise beneath him forced away all sense of personal danger and he knew if he remained inside he would die, so he took a breath and launched himself into midair.

He hit the ground with a terrible jarring of his ankles and he rolled over, aware of shapes scurrying around at the edge of his vision, but not knowing how many in the dark. He fired off another round and thought he might have hit someone, as a shape seemed to fall. With no time to wait and check, he broke into a clumsy run, dodging left and right, making for whatever cover he could find as several more shots rang out.

The drop from the bunkhouse-cum-barn was a matter of maybe ten or twelve feet, but the awkwardness of his landing had turned his ankles and the pain made him sick. Swallowing it down, he picked out a nearby open wagon, lit up orange against the night by the raging flames around him, and scrambled behind it.

Pressing himself up against the side of the wagon, taking in great gulps of air, he took a chance to glance across to the burning bunkhouse. He caught sight of Cross, silhouetted against the flames, preparing to jump, and watched in open-mouthed horror as the first bullets slapped into the man's body. The heavy pieces of lead threw the Federal agent backwards, to disappear once more into the interior of the burning hell that was now the bunkhouse. Agonising moments later, Cross appeared again in the hatch, body bent double as he attempted to climb through and make good his escape from the roaring inferno. As he hooked a leg over the sill, without warning the whole of that side of the wall gave way and he crashed down with it in a great explosion of burning timber, ignited straw and huge plumes of black, gouting smoke.

Instinctively, Simms snapped his face away from the fallout of wood and flame. But he didn't need to look. The horrific noise resulting from the building's collapse brought with it the absolute certainty that Cross lay dead amongst the smouldering ruins.

No one could survive such a fall, in such circumstances.

Cursing, teeth clenched, Simms loomed up from behind the wagon and instantly spotted the men standing out in the open, reloading their rifles, backlit by the brilliant red glow of the flames. With them all revealed, he shot the first in the head from behind the cover of the wagon before stepping out to put his last remaining shot into the second man's chest.

The third, a bull of man, squat, square shouldered, features in deep shadow, turned, his revolver belching fire.

Fear brings with it panic.

Paralysing terror must have gripped the man, for each of the ill-aimed shots missed their mark. He squawked in fear, fumbling for ball and powder. Despite the shadows, Simms knew who this man was, his shape unmistakeable. He looked across the ground to where Cross's revolver lay, stooped down and picked it up.

Straightening, Simms took careful aim.

The two of them looked into one another's eyes, the shadows of the flames dancing across each of their faces.

Simms, without fear.

Magee, a quivering wreck, barely able to stand.

"You miserable bastard," said Simms and shot Magee through the head.

Twenty-Nine

In the town of Twin Buttes, the sun, a blood-red orb, came over the horizon like the harbinger of something dreadful, mused Dixon, stretching his arms as he stood next to the river. Within those first few moments, a pulse of heat travelled across the land like a living thing and hit him full in the face. Beads of sweat burst out across his forehead and he cursed, swinging away to make his way to the water's edge, where he swilled his face to revitalise himself, gasping with relief.

From behind him he heard the unmistakeable snap of a branch, the sound amplified in that still place, where not even the gentle passing of the river could disturb the almost cathedral-like quiet.

Dixon eased himself around on his haunches, hand going to the gun in his waistband. He scanned the tree line opposite, half expecting a band of war-painted Indian warriors to burst forward, but there was nothing. Allowing the tension to slip from his shoulders, he stood up and moved over to the ramshackle old hut, which had served them as shelter for the night before.

Rupert lay curled up under a threadbare blanket, but of Constance there was no sign. Seized by panic, he whirled and ran outside again, gun in hand, now sure of what the sound in the trees had been.

He waited, holding his breath, straining to hear the slightest stirring amongst the undergrowth.

There was nothing.

He started when Rupert yawned behind him. "Dear God, boy, shut the hell up," he snapped, and immediately regretted his outburst when a terrified look crossed young Rupert's face. "I'm sorry. Sorry." He reached out his hand and ruffled the boy's hair.

"What's happened?"

"Your sister." Dixon used his revolver to point towards the trees. "She's gone."

"Where to?" Rupert moved forward on his hands and knees and stood up in the open. He stretched out his limbs and wandered over to the cold remnants of the campfire.

"I don't know," answered Dixon.

"She won't be long, surely. Connie wouldn't just leave."

"No. You're right. Maybe she has gone into town to get some supplies."

"Maybe. Is it dangerous?"

"No. The route back into town is clear. Indians don't roam this way. At least . . . " He narrowed his eyes. "The lack of rain could bring them this way, to hunt for game in the woods."

They exchanged a look.

"She wouldn't know that," said Rupert, his voice sounding frightened.

Dixon grew tense as a sudden, unshakeable sense of unease gripped him. "Get your boots on, we're going after her."

Silas came down the steps from his office and caught hold of the reins, helping Constance down from her horse.

"You're out here early, Miss."

"I wanted to get to the store before they sold out of bacon."

"Ah, aiming to fix breakfast, is that it?"

"I also need to speak with you, Sheriff."

Silas grunted. "Before Dixon woke up, you mean?"

She nodded, brushed off her skirt and motioned for him to go inside the office. He didn't wait to be asked.

Inside, he poured out two cups of coffee and handed her one. She made a face as the bitter taste hit her tongue and replaced the tin cup carefully back on the top of the iron stove.

"So," said Silas, sipping his coffee with relish. "What is it you're wanting to know."

"Did he kill her?"

The sheriff stopped, hand poised, preparing to put the cup to his lip. Slowly putting the cup down, he studied it for a moment before asking, "The girl. Sarah Milligan?"

"You seemed convinced he did it, despite his story which, on the face of it, sounds plausible."

His yes came up and stared at her. "How old are you?"

She blinked. "I beg your pardon?"

"You seem awful astute for one so young. How old are you – seventeen?"

"I am fifteen."

"Dear god. What in tarnation is a fifteen year old doing out here in this hell-hole?"

"We were travelling across to Salt Lake, my father, brother and me, together with our friends. Cholera struck us."

"Damn," Silas shook his head, averting his eyes, her stare hard and uncompromising. "I'm sorry to hear that."

"My father reacted well at first, but his heart gave out the very night after his friends died."

"So you're orphans?"

She swallowed at the mention of the word and for the first time, Silas saw her resolve wavering. "Yes. Rupert and I."

"So, that's what Dixon is doing with you? He is your guardian, of sorts?"

"Not at all. We came across Mr. Dixon on our journey. He was close to death, having suffered a dreadful attack from Indians."

"You – you nursed him back to health?"

"Mrs Morris – Arabella – yes, she nursed him and he recovered. He is so strong."

"Indeed he is. Simms left him for dead, I know that much."

"But why would this Simms shoot him, leave him to suffer?"

"That's what I pondered on for so long. It is my belief, Miss, that Simms sought some form of revenge or retribution for what Dixon had done to Miss Milligan."

"So ... He'd murdered her?"

Silas nodded. "He had a claim to the silver mine her father had discovered. I remember him standing right here, in front of this desk, asking me to witness his signature."

"My God..." She turned away, absently wandering over to the jail cell. "I have to tell you something." She turned around. "We met some other travellers on our way here, spent the night in their company. One of them was an old man with whom Mr. Dixon grew friendly. They spent the night drinking from a whisky jar."

"Well, there's no law against that around these parts if that's—"

Constance held up a hand to cut him off. "He had a gun. A pistol. Mr. Dixon had mentioned more than once he needed such a firearm in case of attack. Only my father owned a revolver; Mr. Morris an old carbine. The old man, he retired to his wagon, leaving Mr. Dixon to finish off the whisky." She pulled in a deep breath. "The old man was found dead the following morning and Mr. Dixon, he..." She turned away again.

"He had the gun."

"I believe he murdered that old man, with all the cold-heartedness of a rattlesnake."

"Well, rattlers may be a lot of things, but they ain't cold-hearted. They only kill to eat, or defend themselves. I'd say Dixon did neither of those things, which means he's a darn sight more dangerous than any snake."

"In my mind, it seems more than passing strange that he should be in such close proximity to two deaths."

"Oh, he's been closer to a lot more than two, Miss. The man is a killer, and that is a statement of fact. The problem I have is proving he had anything to do with Sarah's death."

"He denied killing that old man when I confronted him."

"Darn it, you have some sand, Miss, to do such a thing."

"I have to say, despite all I have said, at no moment have I ever felt afraid in his presence."

Silas raised his brows. "Now, that *does* surprise me. I have been close to many men who were hard-boiled and capable, but not many have made me feel such—"

The door to the jail flew open and one of the two young deputies who accompanied Silas the day before, blasted into the office.

"What in the hell?" said Silas, jumping off his desk, startled.

"There's been a killing."

Both Silas and Constance gaped.

"A *killing*? What in the name of calamity are you talking about, boy?"

"Old Augustus. He's been found dead by his young assistant, a knife buried deep in his chest."

Silas fell back onto his desk and Constance looked across, her lips trembling. "I said I wasn't afraid, Sheriff, but I am now."

Thirty

Pulling his horse up sharply, Simms gazed across his land towards the lone ranch house and knew something was wrong. He could not see the string of horses, which he had accumulated with such care and patience, corralled in the far field, as they usually were. He reached behind him and pulled out the German field glasses from their cracked leather case and focused in on the ranch. Slowly he surveyed the vista, sweeping from left to right and back again. Nothing stirred.

He stopped, senses alert and quickly swung the glasses back over to the right. A thin cloud of dark grey dust moving across the horizon, the distant mountains forming a perfect backdrop, bringing the smudge into sharp focus. Riders.

Another look back to the house. The door hung open. The well, in the front yard, the bucket tied up, seeming to stir in the heat haze. But more than that. Something...

Pulling away the glasses, he wiped the sweat from his eyes with the back of his hand and looked again.

There was something not right about the well. Not the circular stonewall, built maybe two centuries ago by Spanish settlers. Not the cross beam, the rope wound taut. Not the bucket.

Something else.

Then he saw it and he sucked in a sharp breath.

A slight bulge on the far side.

A person, kneeling there, the only part visible the right hind quarters.

Someone knelt there, waiting.

Moving quickly now, he put the glasses back into the case and pulled out the Colt Root rifle sheathed next to the saddle. He checked it then slid from his horse. Tying the reins to a nearby clump of sage, he made his way towards the ranch, loping across the ground, bent double, eyes locked in on the well.

Twenty paces away, he dropped behind a clump of rocks, some taller than a man, others nothing more than pebbles. They afforded him good cover. He rested the rifle over one of them and squinted down the barrel.

The shape behind the well remained still. Simms questioned whether his initial assumption was correct and wished he had brought the field glasses to check.

And then the shape moved, and he knew.

A shadow in the doorway caught his eye. White Dove, standing there, dressed in buckskin trousers and tied-up checked shirt. His heart lurched, her beauty even from this distance breathtaking. In her hand, she held a carbine. He couldn't make out the model, but the fact she held it meant there was danger. But danger from who, from where?

Another quick glance towards the well. Not the figure surely. From her viewpoint, she could clearly see who it was. A friend.

Martinson? Deep Water?

He decided to stand up to his full height, sending out a single, piercing whistle. In the still, silent air, it sounded like an army bugle ordering the battle charge. White Dove immediately went into a crouch, carbine swinging up. Simms waved both arms.

She saw him, and he grinned back at her, their eyes covering the distance between them, recognition sending a pulse of love and relief across the ground.

He broke away from the cover, running hard, aware of the riders way over to his right.

Deep Water rolled over, his revolver coming up and Simms threw up his arms. "Hold fire, old friend."

Deep Water gaped and sat up, a hundred or more questions flashing across his bewildered face. But time was not on their side and Simms continued running over to the house, straight into White Dove's arms and for one brief, wonderful moment, nothing else mattered in the entire world except that they were together again.

He kissed her and gazed down into her huge, dark eyes.

"What the hell is going on?"

She shook her head, pointing to the riders. "They came two days ago, demanding we sign over the ranch."

"They did *what*?" Simms looked in the direction of the steadily approaching men. There were four of them, no longer a shimmering mirage, but clearly distinctive shapes. Tall men on tall horses, cantering with nonchalant ease across the plain. "Who are they?"

"They did not say. They wanted you to sign a deed, giving over the rights to the ranch."

"What – what happened?"

"Martinson refused. So they went away, saying they would return in two days." She held his face in her hands. "Today."

Nodding, Simms smiled down at her. He kissed her again. "Get behind the door and use that carbine if you need to. Where's Martinson now?"

"He is out back, with the horses. We did not want them stampeding if any shooting started."

"You should be out back too."

"No. My place is here. In our house."

"Damn it if you ain't the most beautiful woman I've ever known."

They smiled into one another's eyes once again, for one wonderful moment. But only a moment.

He swung around and stepped out into the open. He shot a glance towards Deep Water. "Take this," he said, sauntering towards the Indian scout. He threw him the Root rifle. "You never were much good with a handgun." He watched Deep Water check the chambers. There were five shots, more than enough for a man of Deep Water's abilities. "I meant to say thanks for what you did back in the fort. Putting down those two soldier boys. Fine shooting," he grinned, "for a Redskin."

"I thought you needed the help, you being such a weak and helpless white boy."

Simms took in a deep breath and pulled back his coat, revealing the Navy at his hip. "Well, now's the time to see just how weak and helpless I really am."

The four riders, so tall and straight in their saddles, crossed the land, slowing down as they drew closer. Simms viewed them with a degree of detachment, arm loose by his side, eyes unblinking, taking in the demeanour of each rider in turn, assessing them, searching for the signs which would lead him to singling out the leader – the most dangerous.

Drawing up to a halt, a man in a long frock coat edged forward slightly, tight lipped, a bead of sweat rolling down from under the brim of his tall, black hat. "You would be Mr. Simms."

"You're on my land and you are uninvited."

The man recoiled a little, whilst those next to him shifted, one of them chuckling softly. "Well, that's the reason we're here, Mr. Simms. To talk, about this land."

"My land."

The man smiled. His right hand came up slowly, palm facing. "I have something you may be interested in." Taking his time, he dipped into his coat and produced a folded-up piece of paper. "This is a bill of sale, Mr. Simms, one which I think you may be—"

"Who sent you?"

The question caught the man a little off-guard. He frowned, titling his head slightly. "I beg your pardon?"

"Who sent you?"

"Mr. Simms, I'm not quite sure if that is relevant. What *is* relevant is that you sign this bill of sale – I assume you *can* read and write?"

"You are one arrogant sonofabitch."

One of the men took in a sharp breath; another chuckled. The face of the man in the frock-coat paled. "I don't think you quite understand the importance of what I'm trying to convey to you, Simms. I want you to sign this document. It is a good price. You won't get any better."

"I ain't selling."

They all chuckled this time, save for the one on the end, a lean-framed individual with black, unfeeling eyes. He wore two guns, holstered at his hips. His saddle creaked as he leaned forward. "Mister, my advice to you would be to sign. Now."

Simms gave him a cursory glance before returning his stare directly towards the man with the paper and the frock-coat. "I ain't selling."

"Now, Mister Simms," said the frock-coat, "that's not really the attitude I'm looking for. This is a good deal, but if you continue to refuse …"

Simms sighed. It seemed the only answer worth his time.

"We said you had two days," continued the man, folding up the paper and returning it to his coat pocket. "Those two days are up. Sign."

"You can turn around and go back to wherever it is you came from. This discussion is over."

"No it ain't," said the lean one on the end.

"Do you even know who I am?"

The lean one smiled. "No, and I don't rightly care."

"Well, you should."

"Oh?" He looked to his colleagues for a glimmer of support, but something had changed about them, their former arrogance and confidence seeping away. The man paused, a slight frown creasing his face, something like self-doubt developing in his features. Turning to Simms, puckering his lips, he said, "All right – so, just who are you, mister?"

"Turn around, or find out."

The air grew still, the distant mountains looming closer, the sky pressing down, heat like a hammer, the arid ground its anvil.

A metallic click of a gun cocking rang like a thunderclap in the heavy atmosphere.

The lean man's eyes flickered towards the well, lips parting slightly, tongue resting on his bottom lip.

He went for his gun in a blur, but Simms moved faster, right hand coming up with the Navy, shooting the lean man in the chest, throwing him off the horse.

In a blink, two more shots rang out and the other two men with guns reared up, the head of one blown apart by a single blast, the other spilling from his saddle, a smudge of red blood developing on his shoulder. He hit the ground hard, rolled over, a quivering hand reaching for his gun. Simms shot him dead.

With the gunshots echoing across the desert floor to mingle amongst the mountains and finally disappear, the stillness returned.

All save the frock-coat's whimpering, his arms raised, face a ghastly shade of pure, chalk-white.

Simms turned the gun towards frock-coat and eased back the hammer.

"Oh sweet Jesus," blurted frock-coat, the words tumbling out of him, "don't kill me, please, sweet Jesus – I'm only the messenger, I swear to God."

"Who sent you?"

"Moss. It was Moss. I never wanted it all to end like this, I swear to God. Please, don't kill me."

"Well, it has ended, and there's the truth of it. You armed?"

"No sir. Sweet Jesus, I never meant for them to try and—"

"Quit hollering." Simms holstered his gun and looked across to Deep Water, now standing up from behind the well. White Dove was walking towards him. "You need to practise your shooting."

Shaking her head, she went up to him and put her head against his chest. He held her close. "I'm sorry," she said.

"Hush now, it's over."

"Is it?"

"I think so. This part anyway." He looked up to see Martinson emerging from behind the house. The Swede was grinning. "Good to see you, old friend."

Taking his hand, Martinson breath came out in a rush. "When they first came, I swear to God I thought they would kill me."

Nodding over to the three corpses, Simms said, "They won't be killing anyone ever again, that's for sure. I'm taking this gentleman back into town and locking him in a cell. Then I'm going to pay this Moss character a visit."

"You might need help," said Deep Water, the rifle in his hands pointing towards frock-coat.

"His name is Burrows," said Martinson. "Him and his friends came calling the other day, demanding I sign the papers."

Burrows cleared his throat. "They're not my friends."

"They're nobody's friends now," said Simms. He let out a long breath. "I have to settle this, tie up the loose ends." He squeezed White Dove tight. "Then I'll be back. I promise."

Simms took a flat wagon across the plain towards Bovey. A grey tarpaulin covered the bodies of the gunmen, lying in grizzly heaps underneath. Beside him on the bucking seat sat Burrows, gnawing at his fingertips.

"So Moss is buying up all the land around these parts, either through legal means, or threat."

Clearing his throat, Burrows stared across the plain. "What's going to happen to me?"

"Not much, *if* you tell the truth."

"If I do that, Moss will kill me."

"Not on my watch he won't. What's the deal with him and the Senator?"

Burrows gaped. "Shit. You know about that?"

"I don't think it's too difficult to figure, given dear old Major Porter's hand in all of this." Simms turned to the quivering wreck of a man sitting next to him. "So give it up, here and now, Burrows. This land is vast and it is empty. Your friends back here," he jerked his thumb to the bodies, "they are in need of some company, and I'll give it to them if you don't tell me the whole goddamned story."

So Burrows did, without hesitation. It came out in a rush, all of the details of how Moss and Bowen quarrelled over dubious land acquisitions, how Moss made the deal with Porter, how he used Laura Miller to charm her way into young Naomi Hanharan's confidence, getting her to sign away her father's estate, masking it all with the clever ruse of thieves entering the house during the funeral. Simms listened and his guts clenched. Land was the new gold.

"He didn't work alone," continued Burrows breathlessly, "Maine is the instigator in all of this, Mr. Simms, Wilbur Carrington Maine. Moss is the figurehead, given he is clean, never having any brushes with the law."

"Unlike Maine?"

Burrows shook his head and looked away. "I never asked where the money came from, but he seemed to have an endless supply of it. When Bowen started asking questions, demanding a bigger cut – that was when Maine hatched the plan to kill him and make it seem like he was the innocent victim of a robbery. It would have worked, too, if those ingrates who did the killing weren't so damned unreliable."

"Involving Porter was your biggest mistake. He saw the chance of concluding his business with me, and getting personal is never a good idea in any kind of business."

The wagon trundled into the town of Bovey and Simms steered the horse leading it into a side street which, at the end, opened up into a small yard. Burrows gasped. "Oh my God."

Giving a short snigger, Simms jumped down as a thin, black-suited man stepped into the sunlight from a single-storey timber building, wood panelling buckling in the heat, the warped sign above the doorway announcing this as an undertaker's establishment. "Detective," he said.

"Mr Vance." Simms nodded towards the wagon. "Three in the back need putting in the ground. I don't know their names, and it don't matter much. Put 'em all together if you have a mind to and send me the bill when it's done."

He turned, jerking his head for Burrows to follow him across the street.

At his office, Simms pointed to the only other chair and Burrows fell into it, still trembling. "You asked me if I could read and write," he said and Burrows nodded. "Well, now it's my turn to ask you – can you?"

"Of course I can."

Grunting, Simms pulled out a sheaf of papers from the top drawer of his desk, together with a pencil. He laid them down before the other. "You write it down – everything. Then you sign it. It will be used in Moss and Porter's trial. As for Maine … you know where he is?"

"I have never met him."

"That wasn't my question."

"No, I don't know where he is. And I doubt if Moss does either. Maine is something of what might be termed a sleeping partner."

"All right, for the time being I'll concentrate on Moss and that evil bitch Laura Miller."

"Moss used her to help him procure certain property hereabouts. I met her once. A handsome woman."

"Procure certain property. What in the hell does that mean?"

Burrows shrugged. "Her former husband was a doctor. Moss suggested she use the contents of her husband's medicine cabinet to … ease the way, so to speak. Far more preferable to gunplay, which has its dangers." He swallowed hard. "As you so effectively proved, Mr. Simms."

Simms didn't answer. The anger brewed inside. Laura Miller, the lust for wealth greater than her sense of right and wrong. "You write it, all of it, then you'll sit nice and tight in the town jail." He stood up straight. "When you've done, I'll go and pay Mrs Miller a visit. I'll arrest her and bring her back before riding over to Naomi. She has a right to know the details. The news might go some way to lighten her grief. It's clear Mrs. Miller used poison to murder Naomi's father."

He walked over to the open door and leaned against the well, staring out into the street, wondering how he might break everything to Naomi, all the while knowing that, no matter how he shaped the words, nothing could ever undo the hurt and anguish she already felt.

Thirty-One

By the time Dixon and Rupert reached the town's main street, both of them were close to collapse. Forced to walk all the way from the camp, and with little shade to protect them, they drained the last of the water from their canteens and stumbled into the saloon.

A few bedraggled customers turned curious faces towards the doors as the two of them came in. Already the barman was filling up two mugs full of beer. "Not too sure if the boy should be—" he began, but Dixon cut him off by wrenching one of the mugs from his hand and shoving into Rupert's own. Uplifting his own, Dixon drained it in one. Rupert took his time, wincing at first, but eventually finished his too.

"Dear God," said Dixon and leaned back against the bar. He gave off a loud whoop of victory. "Damned if it ain't hot out there. You ever known it hotter?" He eyed the man standing some feet away, who shrugged, shook his head and returned to his drink. "I ain't *ever* known it hotter than this."

"You come a long way?" asked the barman, filling up the jugs once again.

"No," said Dixon, taking the beer and drinking it. Smacking his lips, he belched loudly. "It took us an hour to walk all the way from old Dan Stoakes's claim. An hour that felt like a lifetime, ain't that right, Rupert?"

The boy smiled, nursing his beer in both hands. He took a tentative sip, made a face and replaced the beer on the counter. "I thought we'd die for sure."

"Well, we ain't dead and all we need do now is find your sister." Dixon span on his heels and slapped his palms on the counter. "Bar keeper, two more beers and then we'll go seek her out."

"I don't think I want another one, thank you Mr. Dixon."

The Marshal arched a single eye-brow. "Who said it was for you?" He chuckled.

"Girl, you say?"

It was the man standing some feet away who had, at last, found his voice.

Dixon looked along the bar towards the stranger. "Indeed I did."

"Pretty little thing, wearing a cream coloured dress with tiny little blue flowers all over it?"

"That's Connie," said Rupert, gasping. "My God, she must have—"

Dixon reached out and gripped Rupert by the arm, cutting him off in midflow. His eyes bore into the stranger. "You seen her?"

"I did. I saw her coming into town first thing this morning and heading straight to the Sheriff's office."

Dixon stopped, tongue trailing slowly across his front teeth. "Well, well, well." He forced a chuckle and slowly slipped his hand from Rupert's arm, reached for his beer and drained it. "All right then, Rupert my little friend, seems I have an appointment to keep. Bartender, you watch the boy."

He went to move but Rupert caught his arm, face imploring, eyes big as saucers. "Mr. Dixon. What you gonna do?"

"Something I should've done a long time ago, little friend. Now, you wait here. Old Uncle Dixon won't be too long."

He winked and went outside, leaving Rupert to stand and gaze at the gently swinging bat-wing doors.

"He's coming out of the saloon," said the young deputy. Behind him, Silas pulled down an ancient British cavalry carbine from its rack and checked the load. "Hope this old beauty still works."

Connie, standing rooted to the spot, her back against the cell bars, lips quivering, gazed at him. "What are you going to do, Sheriff?"

"Face him down."

"But if he's half the man you said he is ..."

"I have no choice."

"He's striding down the street like he's a soldier on parade," said the deputy and glanced over to Silas. "Should I go get the rest of the boys?"

"You'd never make it across the street."

"Then what do we do, for God's sake?"

Silas pulled in a long breath. "You step outside and stand still, like a stone statue, you hear. You make no play for your gun. You just keep looking straight at him. You call to him, 'good morning', then beckon him over."

"And what in the hell will you be doin'?"

"I'll be lining up one good shot to take him down," said the sheriff, patting the carbine. "I'll be behind you; you'll block his view. At my signal, you jump to your right and I'll kill him."

"And if you miss?"

"You put six slugs into him from your Colt Navy."

"Jeez, Silas, I don't know if I can—"

"Yes you can. The man's a murdering bastard. I have no doubts he murdered Augustus, just like he murdered Sarah Milligan and that other poor soul Miss Constance here told me about."

"Even so, Sheriff, if we miss... He's a gunfighter, for God's sake."

"Gunfighters get shot too. Now get out there and act real easy."

The young deputy faltered, Adam's apple bobbing up and down violently as he swallowed hard. He took one last look around the tiny office then stepped outside.

"Have you another gun?"

Silas looked at the girl, standing there so sweet in her pristine dress. She should be in school, he thought to himself. "Over in the gun rack, there's an old musket. It's a smooth-bore and ain't that accurate, but if it hits home it'll blow a hole in him the size of a barn door."

"Then that will suffice."

He watched her stride across to the cabinet and pull down the gun. She eased back the hammer and checked there was powder in the priming pan. "It needs more powder," she said.

"In the drawer below the cabinet. But not too much."

She grunted. "You miss, I'll shoot him."

"Are you sure you can?"

"Oh yes, Mr. Sheriff sir, I am sure."

Slowing to a crawl, Dixon eyed the young deputy leaning nonchalantly against a hitching post outside the sheriff's office. Some ten paces away, he stopped. "Howdy."

"Good morning," said the deputy.

A trail of sweat ran down the side of the young man's face. Dixon focused in on it. "Hot, ain't it."

The young man nodded.

"People shouldn't be put in such heat as this. What time you got?"

The deputy frowned, deep in thought for a moment, "I have no idea."

"I don't believe it is even noon yet. Imagine the heat after the sun reaches its zenith."

"It's what?"

"Zen-ith. It means directly above us."

"Oh."

Dixon laughed. "Tell me, is the sheriff about?"

"The sheriff?"

"Yeah, the one who pays your wages. Fat man, big nose. Smells like ripe cheese."

Another frown, deeper this time. The young man shifted position, at last ripping off his neckerchief to dab at his face. "I don't know. Maybe he's at home."

"Maybe he's kneeling down behind you with a big old rifle pointing straight at me?"

The young deputy gaped, Dixon grinned and Silas screamed, "*Now!*"

Unfortunately, Silas's plan didn't go quite as he's expected. Before the deputy took a step, Dixon shot him through the throat and was then rolling over in the dirt as Silas loosed off his only shot from the carbine. It fizzed harmlessly overhead and Dixon put two shots into Silas's head, blowing it apart like a piece of overripe fruit.

With the deputy writhing on the ground clutching at his throat and Silas dead, Dixon got to his feet and his eyes settled on Connie, standing ramrod-still, the musket looking far too big in her tiny hands.

"You aiming on killing me, Connie?"

"I am that."

"Well, you had your chance before," he took a step, stopped and put a bullet through the young deputy's head. His writhing ceased. "None of this was necessary."

"You murdered that old man."

"Who, the livery man?" He chuckled, "Yes, I killed him. He was blackmailing me – or at least he was planning to."

"Blackmailing you?"

"He knew more than he should have."

"Like the fact that you murdered that girl? Sarah Milligan."

"I put her out of her misery, is all."

"Like you did with that old man back in camp."

"I needed his gun."

"So you killed him."

Dixon nodded. He glanced over to Silas, lying in a heap just inside the door to the office. "Sometimes the choice is taken out of your hands, Connie."

"Mine isn't."

"No. It's not."

She squeezed off the shot, the recoil stronger than she expected, and she staggered backwards into the office, clattering painfully against the desk and fell down onto her backside.

Dixon came through the door, still chuckling. "Hell of thing to shoot accurately with a piece of old iron-ware like that. You needed a helluva lot more practise." He kicked away the musket. "You'll have a nasty bruise on your shoulder come morning."

She sat there, gaping at him, her features crumpling as the realisation her young life was drawing to a close hit home. "I don't think I'll be seeing another morning."

"No." He brought up his gun. "I reckon you won't be."

Rupert pressed himself deep into the barkeeper's chest, jumping with every gunshot ringing out from the street beyond the batwing doors.

"Sounds like a musket."

The bartender glared at the old man by the bar. Another man was leaning over the top of the double doors, looking into the street and he shouted over to him, "You see anything, Pete?"

Pete nodded. "I see the one who was in here still standing. He's done for young Vaughn, and Silas too. Shit, it's like a massacre out there. And now he's going inside the Sheriff's office."

"The musket?"

Pete looked over his shoulder. "It was meant for him, but whoever fired it missed."

A single gunshot shattered the silence and Rupert gave a whimper, gripping the bartender's shirt so hard one or two of the buttons popped.

"What the hell ...?"

Pete looked out again and gave a groan. "Oh shit, he's coming back."

The barkeeper looked down at the boy and shot a glance at the old man next to him. "Joe, there's a shotgun behind the bar. Get it and shoot that bastard as he comes through the doors. Pete, I got a pocket revolver upstairs in my room. Go get it and cover the bar from the stairs."

"And what will you do."

"I'll stand here and guard this boy from being shot."

"Holy Christ."

"Move yourself, Pete. And whilst you're at it, say a prayer. For every one of us."

* * *

Dixon took his time, using the under barrel lever as he walked to push home the loaded shots into five of the six cylinders. He might have filled up the sixth with ball and powder, but his routine was machine like. He wished he'd brought the Deans with him, but everything had happened so quickly he'd barely had time to think. Dropping the Navy into its holster, he rolled his shoulder and stepped up to the doors of the saloon.

Pausing just outside, he saw the old man with the shotgun and whirled away as both barrels erupted, blowing both doors off their hinges. Cowering for a moment against the adjacent wall, Dixon heard the unmistakeable breaking of the shotgun and went through with another pause.

The old man saw him, mouth falling open, and died as the first shot hit him between the eyes.

"Mr. Dixon, *no.*"

He saw Rupert struggling in the bartender's arms. "You can't kill him," said the big man.

Dixon cocked his head, frowning. In this mood, he could kill any goddamned thing that moved.

A stair creaked and he looked up just as the bullets started flying. None of them were even close, but he went into a crouch anyway, brought up his gun arm and shot the man coming down the stairs in the gut. He doubled over, losing his balance, fell against the wall and slid down the last few remaining steps. At the foot of the stairs, he lay in a heap, clutching at the wound in his stomach, blood leaking through his fingers. Dixon stood up, took careful aim and blew the man's head apart. He then slowly turned and narrowed his eyes towards the bartender. He cocked his revolver.

"*Please,*" said the bartender, "he's nothing but a child. He's done nothing wrong for God's sake!"

Dixon shot the man high up in the shoulder, spinning him around like a top, exposing Rupert who stood, white-faced, terror-stricken. "Mr. Dixon ..."

"I'm sorry, Rupert," he said, brought up the Colt Navy and eased back the hammer once again.

Thirty-Two

Another early morning, the edge taken off the heat this time with bands of thin, grey clouds stretched across the enormity of the sky. Dixon sat upon his horse, pushed down in his stirrups and lifted himself from the saddle to stretch out his back, the ride through the night causing his joints to ache. He pulled off his neckerchief and tipped water from his canteen over it then wiped his face, pressing the material hard against his skin. He was exhausted, but knew he must go on. The people of Twin Buttes would be gathering a posse by now and his trail would prove easy enough to follow. There were only two choices for him to take: Glory or Bovey. He chose Bovey, knowing it to be the town closest to the Pinkerton's ranch. If Simms was not in town, then he would be home. Either way, Dixon would find him.

Nothing else mattered now, the idea of killing the Pinkerton a constant, throbbing pain behind his eyes, a cancer in his soul, eating away at him, blinding him to any sense of propriety, justice or mercy. Once, his god was money, the pursuit of wealth. His desire for it clouded his judgement, but it gave him strength and determination. When he killed Sarah Milligan, he felt nothing, only the elation of knowing he could finally get his hands on her father's silver mine. But now, now a demon replaced his avarice – revenge. Revenge for what Simms did to him, shooting him, leaving him for dead. He'd visit upon the Pinkerton such a fury, such a world of pain, and he'd enjoy every moment.

Licking his lips, he followed a winding track meandering between high, steep hillsides and made camp in a secluded, well-hidden area. With the day easing by he thought no ill could come of making a fire and he placed his coffee pot upon the embers and listened to the beans percolating inside, thoughts going nowhere, eyes hazy and tired.

Sometime later he woke with a start, instinctively going for his gun, but there was no one there, only the sizzling of the now boiled dry pot. He knocked it off the dying fire with his boot and stood up, peering towards the sky in an attempt to gauge the time. Damn it all, he cursed himself. He needed to sleep, but not now, not with Bovey so close.

He hurriedly packed away the camp, scattering the cinders angrily. His horse snickered, alarmed at the man's sudden aggression. Patting the mare gently across the neck, Dixon hauled himself up into the saddle and urged the animal along the trail once more.

Bovey nestled in a slight dip in the land, a developing town, several new buildings in a state of half-completion with men in overalls labouring at forming cross-beams and applying paint. If prosperity was indeed about to come calling, Dixon's visit might put the brakes on people's optimism, for he knew for certain Simms's presence caused people to look forward to a future full of hope and good fortune. Well, with the Pinkerton dead it wouldn't be any of those things.

He guided his horse down the main street, ignoring the curious looks of the passersby, and tied his horse at the hitching rail outside one of the larger merchant stores. On either side flat wagons stood, tailgates down, ready to receive goods. The town bustled, townsfolk cheery, many stopping to engage in animated conversations. The sun broke out through the clouds every now and then, adding to the overall atmosphere of good cheer. Dixon rolled his tongue around inside his mouth and spat into the dirt. He went into the store.

A gaggle of customers were close to the counter, a large man hefting a pickaxe in his hand, another bending over an order book, signing it with a stubby pencil. Two young girls played with a dressed manikin in the corner, tugging at the dolls' dress, giggling with delight. A handsome woman strode over and chided them, but they continued nevertheless. Dixon turned from them and strode to the counter.

"Cap, ball and powder," he said flatly.

The storekeeper behind the counter gave him a sharp look. "One moment."

The man returned to serving the others. Dixon coughed, leaned over, "That's all I need."

The big man with the pickaxe sighed, "It's all right, Patrick. Serve the gentleman."

Dixon tipped the brim of his hat, ignoring the storekeeper's glare.

Whilst he waited, he laid down his guns on the counter. The Navy, the Adams double-action and the revolver he'd lifted from one of the men in the saloon back at Twin Buttes – a pocket Colt Dragoon.

"That's a lot of hardware you've got there, mister."

Dixon didn't look up. The two men beside him muttered between themselves and Dixon sensed their agitation, their nervousness. The sooner this ghastly business was over with the better.

The storekeeper returned from out back and placed two small boxes on the counter, together with a bulging cloth bag, about the size of a man's palm. Dixon nodded his thanks and set to loading up each of the guns in turn.

No one spoke, mesmerised at the efficiency of Dixon's actions and, when he was finished, he snapped down a few dollar coins, put the Navy into its holster, dropped the Dragoon into his inside coat pocket and, hefting the Adams in his hand, gave them all a nod and strode out.

He stood on the boardwalk and looked down the street. Vaguely aware of the gasps of people as they wandered past him, he thought he recognised the man on a horse leaving the livery stable at the far end of the main drag. Narrowing his eyes to focus in more keenly, he sucked in his breath and jumped down into the dirt, almost colliding with two prim-looking women about to step up into the store. Ignoring their outraged cries, he swung up into the saddle and broke into a canter.

It was Simms. If Dixon had a rifle he could blow him out of the saddle. But he didn't have a rifle, and he cursed his lack of foresight, berating himself for not taking up Silas's old carbine. Moving across the front of a small office, bearing the sign 'Pinkerton Detective Agency' across the front door, he reined in, grinning broadly.

Jumping down from his horse, he stepped up to the office and kicked through the door, the Adams ready.

The room loomed empty. After giving it a cursory glance, Dixon spotted what he needed and crossed to the wall behind the desk. Mounted on hooks was a Halls carbine. He took it down, checked the load and strode outside.

Looking down the street, he saw Simms had gone. Suppressing his annoyance, Dixon mounted up again and moved over to the livery stable to find exactly where the Pinkerton had headed.

The moment for confrontation was at hand.

Thirty-Three

Spring Acres proved nothing like what he imagined. After he escorted a subdued and frightened Laura Miller back to town, he asked the boy at the livery stable for directions to Naomi's new home. He soon found it, a little under an hour's ride away, nestled in a small, wooded valley, a tiny stream running by, the entire property appearing nowhere near as big as its name suggested.

The maid opened the door to him. Here was one thing that hadn't changed. Doffing his hat before taking it off, Simms stepped inside the small, narrow hallway and waited.

Naomi came from out of a side room, looking as handsome as she did on their first meeting, but no longer sad, the pasty pallor now replaced by full lips and a blooming complexion. With her back so straight, her eyes so keen and bright, her determination and courage shone through.

"Thank you for coming by, Detective."

"My pleasure." He cast his eyes around the hallway, "I need to avail you of the facts, Miss Hanharan. The facts concerning the sale of your property."

A single nod and she led him into the parlour, a room barely able to accommodate them both, the furniture too big for such a small space. He lowered himself onto a chair by a window table and, with his hat on his lap, turned the brim through his fingers.

He told her everything, as far as he could, repeating much of what Burrows had conveyed to him, together with his own thoughts and suspicions, most of them confirmed by Laura Miller's testimony. When he finished, he stared down at his feet, feeling suddenly ashamed. "My one regret is I didn't get to the bottom of all of this before Moss took full advantage."

"No need for regrets, Mr Simms. You could not have known. And besides, in a way, I suppose my family have benefitted. We would likely have sold the big house anyway after Daddy passed away."

"Yes, but at a much more realistic price." He coughed. "But ... perhaps he never would have passed away if that harlot had not poisoned him."

She looked at him for a long time and, for a brief moment, a trembling came to her mouth as her proud, unflustered demeanour of just a few minutes ago broke down. He drew in a shuddering breath. "We weren't to know." He saw her lips quivering slightly before she forced a tight smile. "Would you like some tea, Detective?"

"No, thank you. I won't take up any more of your time."

She absently pushed aside the crochet work lying on the sofa next to her. "The town is no doubt alive with what happened. When Betsy goes to fetch some groceries, she'll hear it all, second-hand as always."

"Folk will always gossip, even when they don't know the truth."

"Would they even care if they did?"

"Probably not."

"I never would have thought Mrs Miller could be capable of such a thing."

Simms looked away as he recalled the moment he confronted Laura Miller.

The house was a large, sprawling affair and he took his time to study each of the windows staring back out at him. A white-painted fence enclosed the splendid drive, a horse and carriage standing by the main door, but no other sign of life. Half expecting there to be a small army waiting for him, or any other passing lawman, Simms gently steered his horse around to the rear, alert, ready to draw his gun at the least sign of movement.

Dismounting in the rear yard, his eyes settled on the collection of outhouses, barns and sheds. Nothing stirred. Moving with caution, he approached the rear entrance, turned the handle and stepped inside.

From somewhere within the faint sound of the virginals wafted through the many rooms and corridors. He stood in the kitchen area, a massive oak table before him, giant ovens and a spit over a cold fire, a curious air of abandonment hanging heavily all around.

Through the door, he mounted a set of stone steps and came into the entrance hall. The music sounded closer now and, pausing for a moment to glance towards the other rooms, he headed for the one with its door yawning open.

She sat with her back to him, her delicate fingers caressing the keys, the melody light, almost whimsical. He coughed and she gave a cry, whirling around in her stool.

"Oh my," she gasped, hand coming to her mouth. "Why, Mr. Simms, you scared me."

"My apologies, Mrs Miller."

"Oh please, less of the formalities." She stood up, closing the lid of the tiny instrument. She caressed the delicately patterned woodwork and sighed. "Such a beautiful thing."

"Ma'am, this ain't no social call."

Without turning, she remained silent. He noticed her shoulders slumping, any last dregs of fortitude draining away. "He's not here. He left some hours ago, with a bunch of his men."

"Any idea where he might have gone?"

"To hell for all I care." She turned and there were tears in her eyes. "I know why you are here."

"I expect you do."

"I won't lie to you, Detective. I will tell you everything you want to know. That scoundrel played me for a flighty fool, and now he has gone. I owe him nothing. Nothing at all." So she told him and confirmed all he already knew. Moss and Bowen were in it up to their necks, land deals and false claims, stretching right across to Salt Lake. When Bowen got greedy, Moss, on Maine's behest, had the Senator killed. His only mistake was to rely on Porter to carry out the grizzly deed, Porter who wanted Simms dead so badly it marred his judgement.

Simms pulled himself out of his reverie and smiled across to Naomi Hanrahan, standing there, waiting. "Looks can be deceptive," he said, the irony unmistakable in his voice.

"You knew her?"

"Slightly. She invited me to dinner some time ago."

"And you accepted?"

"No." A tiny chuckle. "I, er, found myself somewhat preoccupied at the time."

"Ah," her eyes glinted with playful impishness. "I have heard you are married, Detective. To a Native lady, so I understand."

"Not, er, married. No."

"Oh." The glint dimmed.

"I am not a religious man, Miss Naomi. Marriage is not the 'honourable estate' it's cracked up to be." He saw her startled look and he quickly added , "In my humble opinion, you understand."

She didn't, and he could see she didn't. Turning away, she reached for a tiny bell and shook it. "Tea, Detective."

Rather than repeating his earlier refusal, he looked out of the window. The garden was tiny and reminded him of similar dwellings back in Illinois. "She will be arrested and stand trial, Miss Naomi. You may be called as a witness."

"Oh. Witness to what?"

He looked at her. "How she was, with your father. I found corroborating evidence. Other witnesses, who will testify. It is almost certainly her that poisoned your father after Moss assured her he was ready to swoop."

"Moss. The land-grabber. I had no suspicion of that, Detective. All I knew was that Daddy was happy and it was Laura Miller who made him happy."

"Yes, whilst at the same time poisoning him with tiny measures of belladonna over a prolonged period. I found the poison in her late husband's medicine cabinet, together with some diary entries she showed me."

"She showed you?"

"She held nothing back. Her hatred for Moss is ..." He shrugged, no further words needed. "The evidence will lead me to the thieves who took your mother's jewellery. I'll bring each and every one else involved to justice, have no fear."

"They were all in it together?"

"Orchestrated by Moss."

"And where is he?"

"I don't know. Not yet. It is my hope Mrs. Miller will divulge more of what she knows and, when she does, I shall track him down."

They stared into one another's eyes for many moments, until at last she pulled in a breath. "You are a dangerous man to know, Detective."

"It's my job."

"Even so."

He grunted. "Even so."

At that point, the maid came in, wiping her hands on a small towel. "You rang, ma'am?"

Pressing her lips together, Naomi shook her head. "I did, but ... No, Betsy, Detective Simms has decided not to have tea and is leaving. Unless there is anything else, Detective?"

She held his eyes as he sighed and stood up. "No. I just wanted to give you a heads up about the likelihood of you being called."

"Yes." She brushed her hands on her apron and stared. This time, she did not offer a handshake. "Goodbye, Detective."

Positioning his hat upon his head, Simms gave a tiny bow and left.

At the door, Betsy touched his arm. "Please, don't be taking her manner too much to heart, sir – she's still grieving."

He smiled in understanding. "Things have been very ... traumatic. But, it's over now. She needs some rest and time to readjust."

Betsy nodded and opened the door for him.

The bullet hit the doorframe with a slap, sending out a shower of splinters. Throwing his arms up to protect his face, Simms bundled himself, together with the maid, into the hallway, flattening them both against the hard floor.

Naomi appeared hands waving, hysterical, "What in the name of the Almighty—"

"*Get down*," roared Simms.

She looked at him, incomprehension written in each furrowed brow and she looked towards the open doorway, "Oh my Dear Lord!"

But she said no more as the bullet tore into her, blowing her backwards against the door of the parlour. She slid sideways, a bright red stain of blood on the paintwork.

The maid screamed, a long, drawn-out wail of despair and fear. Pushing her aside, Simms rolled over onto his back, the Smith and Wesson in his hands, aiming down the sight as the man beyond strode forward, as nonchalant as you like, but his right hand finding difficulty feeding in another cartridge.

Then Simms saw why. The man's first two fingers were missing from his right hand.

The man looked up, his smile turning into a weasel-like leer.

Simms shot him in the chest. The man wavered, looking down at the bloody wound in his gut. His eyes came up, feverish, wild, the pain and shock of the wound causing no reaction whatsoever. He put another round into the Halls carbine, unconcerned, dismissive and swung the gun up and fired.

The blast sang past Simms's head within a whisper. Snarling, Simms sat up, easing off three more rounds from the Smith and Wesson. Two hit the man, one high up in the shoulder, spinning him around, the next in the back. He fell to his knees and the third went over his head.

"Bastard," hissed Simms and got up, throwing away the Model One and whipping out the Navy in its stead.

Stepping out onto the raised boardwalk, he quickly scanned the open ground, checking no one else was there.

Reassured, Simms approached the kneeling man. The Halls fell from unfeeling fingers. He remained motionless.

Kicking away the carbine, Simms stepped around to the man's front and gasped.

"Sweet God Almighty!"

"Thought you'd killed me, eh, Simms?" The man's eyes streamed with tears, a trickle of blood oozed from his mouth.

Marshal Dixon.

"Holy shit," breathed Simms.

"Hate and thoughts of revenge kept me alive, Simms. But I was so desperate to kill you I missed with my first shot." He brought up his shattered right hand, the first two fingers missing from when Simms shot the Marshal back in old Dan Stoakes's silver mine all that time ago. "Makes shooting difficult. You are blessed, you stinking sonofabitch. But my next shot will kill you."

The small, pocket Dragoon appeared from nowhere.

His hand shook. Blood loss and shock at last kicking in.

Simms, anticipating another attack, was faster. The Navy barked once, the bullet going into the Marshal's brain, ending everything right there and then.

The ensuing silence hung there, an epitaph to the dead man's quest for vengeance. Empty. Failed. Then Betsy's screams pierced the air, bringing Simms out of himself and he ran across to the house, taking the steps to the porch in one bound and found the maid in the hallway, cradling Naomi's head in her lap.

"Oh Detective, please. Please help her."

Without a word, he ran into the parlour and whipped up the crochet pad and took it back to the maid, thrusting it into her hand. "Press this against the wound, hard as you can." She looked at him, her blank stare bringing anger to his voice. "Just *do it, goddamnit!*"

Simms showed her, putting the pad against the blood filled-cavity in Naomi's left side. Closing his eyes, he gritted his teeth. "Hold it and do not let go. I'm riding over to Doc Jeffries in town. I'll be back with him, as soon as I can. You do not ease up on the pressure, you hear."

"She's gonna die."

He made no reply, but knew the truth of it. Yes, she was going to die. Simms, the veteran of so many deaths, knew there could only be one outcome from such a wound, but he merely squeezed the maid's hand, saying, "Keep pressing," and then he was gone.

Thirty-Four

A small knot of people stood around the open grave as four men lowered the coffin carefully into the ground. The preacher read the last prayer and Simms turned away, hat remaining in his hands, and looked down towards the town of Bovey.

"It looks almost peaceful from up here."

Simms looked askance at Martinson and grunted. "I wonder if it ever will know the true meaning of peace."

"It's over now, my friend. Dixon, everything he stood for, every malicious, vindictive act, ended. All thanks to you."

"He still managed to do what he did." Simms sighed, studying his hat for a few moments. "I wonder how many more there are like Dixon out there, lurking in the shadows, biding their time in broken-down old saloons, planning and scheming."

"Perhaps men like Moss will replace men such as Dixon."

"Not for some while, I think. Moss is a different kind of criminal, but he's just as dangerous. At least with vermin such as Dixon, you know where you stand. Moss ..." He shook his head, "his kind, they smile as they bury the knife deep."

"Usually in your back."

Simms gave a short snigger. "Yeah, that too."

"But Moss is behind bars – you saw to that."

Simms nodded. Hunting the man down had not proven difficult, the man's arrogance being his undoing, believing nobody would dare testify against him. When confronted with the reality, he sank into himself and admitted everything. "And he'll stay there too. With Porter's evidence, I reckon he will probably never see daylight again."

"They might hang him."

"Maybe. Maybe not. He still has powerful friends, and his partner, Maine, he's still out there applying his influence."

"And Porter will tell it as it truly was?"

"Oh yes, Brewster's testimony will see to that. And Burrows too. No, the weight of evidence is too great for any of them to escape justice, certainly not Moss. Laura herself will be shut away. Sad. A woman like that, to be lured into such a scheme."

"Moss had a way with women?"

"It would appear so." He shook his head, reflecting on a moment, not so very long ago, when Laura Miller stepped into his office and offered to make him dinner one evening. If he tried hard enough he could still taste the moist, delicious cornbread she's made. "Damn... a woman like that." Taking in a deep breath, he carefully replaced his hat on his head. "I've been assured Brewster's sentence will be commuted, just as I promised. Even so, he'll face a dozen years hard labour. All in all, I think I can call this case closed."

"Until the next one."

A thin smile spread across Simms's face. "For now, all I want to dwell on is a long rest, down in my ranch." He winked. "With White Dove."

And, with both men smiling broadly, they wandered down the path, which led to Bovey whilst behind them, the mourners gave up one last, final prayer for Naomi Hanharan.

The End

Dear reader,

We hope you enjoyed reading *Blood Rise*. Please take a moment to leave a review, even if it's a short one. Your opinion is important to us.

Discover more books by Stuart G. Yates at https://www.nextchapter.pub/authors/stuart-g-yates

Want to know when one of our books is free or discounted for Kindle? Join the newsletter at http://eepurl.com/bqqB3H

Best regards,

Stuart G. Yates and the Next Chapter Team

You might also like:
Bloody Reasons by Stuart G. Yates

To read the first chapter for free, head to:
https://www.nextchapter.pub/books/bloody-reasons

About the Author

Stuart G Yates is the author of a eclectic mix of books, ranging from historical fiction through to contemporary thrillers. Hailing from Merseyside, he now lives in southern Spain, where he teaches history, but dreams of living on a narrowboat in Shropshire.